SILENT ACCUSATION

SILENT ACCUSATION

LESLEY SCOTT

The Book Guild Ltd

First published in Great Britain in 2023 by
The Book Guild Ltd
Unit E2 Airfield Business Park,
Harrison Road, Market Harborough,
Leicestershire. LE16 7UL
Tel: 0116 2792299
www.bookguild.co.uk
Email: info@bookguild.co.uk
Twitter: @bookguild

Typeset in 11pt Adobe Garamond Pro

Printed and bound by CPI Group (UK) Ltd, Croydon, CR0 4YY

ISBN 978 1915352 422

British Library Cataloguing in Publication Data.
A catalogue record for this book is available from the British Library.

For Clee, Connie, Thomas and Caitlin

ONE

The darkening London sky brought a sense of premature lateness, amplified by our early escape from work. It was mid-December 1982, and I walked out of Henry's restaurant with my boss, Philip Wallis, into a sharp afternoon. Our long, winter coats covered made-to-measure suits and through a leather glove, he shook my hand.

'See you tomorrow, Peter.'

'Thanks, Philip. I mean, thank you for everything.'

'You better be worth it.' He slapped me on the back and strode off to Charring Cross.

He'd offered me his top client portfolio, with the promise of promotion and a bonus cheque to match. Thatcher would have clapped. And I had no doubts that I *was* worth it. Despite every ache of my unloved being, I knew that I shone and belonged with Philip.

The afternoon had been a loose one. I'd gossiped on my peers after only the slightest pressure. But only essential stuff that Philip needed a handle on, of course. Then Philip had dropped his bombshell. The partners were impressed, my talent was precious and their show of appreciation enticing enough to stop me from straying. In front of Philip, I'd contained myself, I'd smothered my excitement and now I needed to walk and burn it off.

I weaved my way through the Covent Garden Christmas shoppers, armed with lethal carrier bags, determined in their paths. My footsteps echoed through St Martin's littered alley, where I ignored the two homeless men in their nests of sleeping bags. Then over the main road I danced between the traffic, threading my way to a pulsing Leicester Square. I stopped and took a breath to quell the brandy and champagne. There was something I could sense, something weirdly different. An awakening in the cinema lights of Ben Kingsley's *Ghandi*. A heightening of the senses in the roasting chestnut smoke. Then a busker struck guitar strings to the "Eye of the Tiger", and for winning my attention, I flipped him fifty pence.

The streets became emptier as I cut through side lanes and passed a row of shops that glowed festive in the gloom. Glass cases of shiny, delicious chocolate led on to toys and children's clothing. A window full of fairy lights showed Christmas cards and gifts. Then I was drawn to a shopfront of bright Georgian windows, where second-hand books beckoned from their shelves.

I stepped in and the fusty smell of ripe pages hit me as hard as the skewed ratio of books to workable space. Tall cases lined the walls, all full to bursting, with overflows of books sat double on most shelves. Boxes and crates filled the floor with no care for health and safety or the presentation of the place. I stepped around a carousel of Penguin Classics and tried to orientate myself. At the back of the shop, hiding in the corner, a man in a diamond-patterned jumper sat reading behind a desk.

'Afternoon,' I said in my cheeriest greeting.

He looked up but then his eyes dropped back to his paper. I raised an eyebrow in response to his non-existent welcome and headed for the shelves.

2

A crimson-red guidebook on Chile caught my eye, but as I slipped it out, its neighbour slid out too. I grabbed out instinctively, saving the book from falling, and found myself holding a small, black hardback. I read its title, *The Silent Accusation*, just as raised voices came from behind. A man was at the counter, arguing for a refund, and Mr Diamond-Patterned jumper was refusing to consent. I didn't fancy the customer's chances and before long my judgement proved right. After another firm refusal, the customer started shouting and, uncomfortable with the tension, I left.

Back on the street, the night sky had fallen, and the chill pierced through my coat. I walked out of the lane and searched for a taxi home. A couple whizzed straight past, but after a minute, I saw another and waved to flag it down. The driver carved an exaggerated arc to the pavement and with the grace of a tiger I pounced in.

'Randall Terrace, Islington,' I called.

'Islington, righty-o.' He looked over his shoulder and manoeuvred into the road.

I slipped back on the hard, leather seat and my heart dropped when I thought I'd lost my briefcase, until I remembered I'd locked it in my desk. I'd guessed right: I didn't feel like work after a lunch with Philip; my head was in no fit state. I replayed our conversation, and a thrill sprang through my body with the thought of my impending promotion. I'd be earning more at twenty-five than my father had at sixty, and I cracked my fingers as I considered how that felt. Somehow, there was no satisfying roar of victory, just a half-hearted cheer for an empty success. My swagger melted with that single train of thought and for a moment I felt vulnerable and trivial and lost.

I shook the sentiment away and caught my reflection in the passenger window. I traced a finger along my temple and

3

as I smoothed down my hair, caught the driver watching in his rear-view mirror. Our eyes locked for a moment, his dead, flat stare betraying neither interest or contempt. Then he broke the exchange and turned his eyes back to the road. When I followed his gaze, we were nearly at my flat.

I clambered out and dipped into my pocket for the fare. Instead, I found a small, black book. I stared at it, trying to place why it was there.

'That's three-pound-sixty.' The driver broke my thoughts and I fished into my pocket again.

'Here's a fiver, keep the change.'

'Brilliant, mate, thank you.'

In the fug of his parting fumes, I re-appraised my loot. It didn't merit the effort of a trip to return it, so I pocketed the book and turned home.

The Edwardian terrace was now three apartments, spread over four floors. Bob and Diane, a retired couple, had the ground floor and basement. Isha, a bank executive for Lloyds, lived alone on the first floor. And I had the pleasure of the draughty attic. My finances had outgrown the place and I deserved something smarter, but moving required energy that I never seemed to have.

My shoes clacked up the bare wooden staircase and past the silent first floor. I pressed up the last flight and, on the tight square of landing, slotted in my key. I snapped on my lights to show a cubbyhole lobby, the space overtaken by a crowded coat stand. Then next a basic lounge with its worn-out, rented furniture – a beige, two-seater sofa and burgundy armchair, a fifties, mahogany sideboard and a Formica coffee table.

With a hard click, I turned on the gas fire and, in its instant kick of heat, braved unbuttoning my coat. Remembering the book, I pulled it from my pocket and

4

balanced it on the arm of the chair. Then with a smooth swing, I threw my coat over the sofa, unthreaded my scarf and cast it onto the seat. I looked at the creasing pile of cashmere and, thinking better of it, folded the soft fabric neat.

Last night's glass still sat on the coffee table, and I picked it up and blew in it to clear out any dust. From the sideboard cupboard, I grabbed the whisky and poured out a tot. The liquid tickled my lips as its warmth spread down my throat, and when it caught my breath, I sputtered a little cough.

I flopped into the armchair, the springs complaining against the stretch and the fake velvet so cold that it felt damp through my trousers. I kicked off my shoes, swung my feet onto the table and closed my eyes for a moment. My head tipped forward and in reflex I snapped it back, but then I could hear my own snoring. Drowning in exhaustion, I let my body flop.

A noise sounded in the background of my senses and, coming round, I heard a rap.

'Hailstones,' I mumbled, and after rubbing my eyes, I saw the book had fallen onto the floor. Its twisted body had spat something from its pages and, curious, I picked it up. I held a yellowing, handwritten business card. On one side there was a name and address: 'Mr & Mrs E H Featherstone, 15 Dawson Road, Kensington'. On the flip side was a line of writing. I struggled to read the scrawl but took each word in turn, deciphering its meaning by making sense of it with the word before.

'Find me in death – bye, bye.'

A draught blew across my neck, and I shivered. I stuffed the card back into the pages and squeezed the book tight shut. The title's gold letters gleamed in contrast to the matt-black cover, and I considered the meaning of *The Silent*

Accusation. My brain was too tired to unravel it, or to read so much as a page. Whoever it was silently accusing, judgement would have to wait.

TWO

'What do you think he'll say when he sees them?' I ask Mum again. We're watching TV in the lounge, waiting for Dad to get home.

She smiles and rubs my hair. 'He'll be ecstatic. He'll want to tell your nan.'

'He won't miss them, will he?'

'Stop fussing, silly. He *always* checks for post. He's not going to change the habit of a lifetime.' We giggle in shared excitement. 'Six grade As! He'll be *so* pleased.'

The minutes take hours to pass, and when his key grates in the lock, my heart thumps. He steps inside and shuffles off his coat, hanging it on the rack. There are long seconds of envelopes being torn open and our stifled laughter almost gives the game away. We sit, desperate to cash in on our trick.

He walks in, standing tall in his Savile Row suit, his full head of ash hair still neat from the morning and the permanent sneer almost gone from his lips. 'I see you have your results.'

He looks me in the eye and for an instant, I feel something there. But there's not another word. He picks up the paper, walks out of the lounge and I hear him going upstairs.

Mum watches my face and nudges me, rolling her eyes to say, 'Typical him.' My moment is already over, my heart crushed and ready to spill.

I pushed away the memory with the throw of the sheets. The sting of a wet shave grounded my emotions and after a tussle to flatten my nut-brown hair, I armed myself in a charcoal suit with a crisp white shirt and red silk tie. In the lobby, I pulled on my overcoat, drained my coffee cup and left.

With promotion looming, work had new purpose, and in the sanctuary of my office, I planned my day. It was the best space in the building, newly refurbished with poster art, white walls and bamboo blinds. Thrown out was the old mahogany furniture, replaced with a white, ergonomic, curve-topped desk. I moulded myself into the high-backed leather chair and sketched out a list with my silver Montblanc pen.

Around eight-thirty, Ajay, my second in command, dropped by with coffee. Ajay had come to Montgomery's straight from school, a smart kid who wanted to earn some serious money. Seeing something in him, Philip had given him a chance, and like me he had risen through the ranks. Now he was gunning for his next promotion and was keen to follow my lead. I enjoyed his confidence and cheeky sense of humour; he was a sound addition to the team.

The coffee fuelled my morning while I dabbled in Japanese electronics and saw several assets rise throughout the day. However, one of my juniors hadn't fared so well. Ignoring the analysts, he'd listened only to his ego and cashed in a profit, only to see the shares soar stratospherically at the last gasp of play. His clients and the company had missed out on thousands. That was okay for amateurs but inconceivable at Montgomery's. Before I could come down on him, the team waded in.

'Don't worry Tim.' Ajay poked first. 'Dave Green made that mistake.'

'Who the hell's Dave Green?' Naïve Tim swallowed the bait.

'He cleans the loos.' Laughter broke across the team and Ajay grinned at his own comic timing.

'Go fuck yourself.'

'No need for that, Timothy.' Helen, my next senior broker, wagged a playful finger. 'You'll get a nice uniform and rubber gloves to match.'

'Although the vacancy is for the ladies' loo,' added team-mate Dan.

'Now, seriously…' Ajay leaned on Tim's desk.

'*Seriously*, all of you, just fuck off!' Despite the team's jokes, Tim knew his loss could be fatal.

'I'm trying to help you,' said Ajay.

'What, by being an arse?'

'No. Go wipe your nose… and then I'll write you a reference.' Tim checked Ajay's expression. 'Won't be good, though.'

To the team's amusement, Tim snapped up from his desk and stormed out.

'Nice one, chaps. Incredibly supportive,' I shouted from my office. 'And thanks for making my job harder.' Tim was definitely in trouble; I was deciding how much.

'Ah, he'll live,' Ajay said as he crossed back to his desk.

'In exile, in Siberia,' junior Steve added to more laughs.

I remembered the pain of the early days. Defending the underdog would get your manhood questioned, and I'd had enough of that from my father. To distance myself,

I'd worked non-stop – arriving earliest to prepare, staying latest to cold call and sacrificing every Saturday. Labour not luck generated my early breaks and Philip soon noticed. What began as a summer job, helping with filing and photocopying, grew into trading and finding my passion. I may not have been popular with the drinking crowd, but I didn't need them for promotion. As a supervisor, I controlled my time, carving a path straight to Team Leader and bringing me ever closer to the boss. There our symbiosis grew – me dependent on every drop of Philip's praise and him hooked on exploiting my devotion.

Of course, keeping my new spiritual home meant leaving university. It was a step too far for my father, whom I'd already shamed by being the first male Tyler to not get into Cambridge. He'd saved face by bragging about his son at 'progressive' Bristol, selling his false pride to the point of no return. When I dropped out, his minute bit of tolerance died. But all my chips were in and I knew that in time, I would make the ice man proud.

Focusing back on work, I picked up the phone, but before I had the chance to dial, Philip bounded in. As usual, he looked freshly dressed and shaven, and smelt like cedar and forest rain. At fifty-two he was still the company's squash champion, a man who had no time for people any less than perfect. He rapped three times on my desk.

'This weekend's going to be a grind.' A crumb of a smile gave away his mischief.

'I'm away this weekend, remember. It's Keisha's father's sixtieth.' I'd managed to keep the relationship for a whole four months and didn't plan on losing it yet.

'Ah yes, but this is Shelltec. I told you, we need to go through absolutely everything and confirm the forecast before Monday. We'll start Saturday around nine.'

'I thought Ajay had offered—'

'Come on, Peter. Ajay's keen, but he's not you.' I looked out and saw Ajay talking with Helen, both oblivious to my pain.

'I can't do this without you. She'll understand. Go another weekend when things aren't so tight. You can't say no to Shelltec.'

There was no use arguing; Philip would have his way. And I needed to give in to him willingly, to show him I was his.

'Okay.' I looked him in the eye, serious about his request. 'It won't be easy, but I'll rearrange.'

'Good man.' He never doubted it.

I seethed inside and my stomach sank at the thought of telling Keisha. At such unreasonably short notice it would spoil her whole weekend. As well as meeting her parents, a host of relatives were flying over from Jamaica – aunties, cousins and uncles that she was keen for me to meet. I wanted to get the deed over with but then remembered she was out Christmas shopping. Making a mental note to call later, I flicked open a file and distracted the pain with work.

As an hour ticked by, the office emptied, leaving the main floor in darkness. I was semi-aware that I should call it a day, when I remembered to phone Keisha. Feeling like a condemned man, I dialled her number, secretly hoping she'd be out. I gnawed at my thumbnail until she answered.

'Hi, it's me.'

'Hello, you. This is a lovely surprise. I wasn't expecting to hear from you until the morning.' She was all warmth and high spirits and didn't deserve disappointment.

'How was the shopping?'

'It was good thanks. I got Dad's birthday stuff, which was the main thing. What about you, have you packed?'

'No, not yet.' I swallowed. 'Actually, Philip's just—'

'You are still coming.'

'Well…'

'Oh no. This is a joke.'

'Sorry, it's not.'

'Peter!' I could hear the anger rising. 'You can't let me down like this. You must come, everything's arranged. I *can't* go on my own.'

'I'm really, really sorry, but I have no choice. It's an imp—'

'Yes, you do have a choice, Peter. You need to tell Philip no. This is going to be so embarrassing. Everyone's expecting you.'

'I'm really sorry.'

'You're sorry? Thanks a lot!' She slammed down the phone, leaving the dead tone to convey her disgust.

Irritated and defeated, I returned to my file and tried to pick up my thoughts. I read the same paragraph three times until it sank in, determined to end the day on a better note. I'd just forced my head back into it when something shuffled outside my door.

'Hello?'

I listened, but the office was silent, so I went back to my notes. I'd only written three words when the noise happened again.

'Who's there?' I put down my pen, walked to the door and stared into the dark main floor. 'Is somebody here?'

I wondered whether the boys were playing a joke, but this was childish, even for them. I waited a moment and was just about to turn when a scratching on the carpet sounded to my right. I stepped out from the protection of my office walls and inched along until my hand felt a switch. The lights blinked on to show I was alone.

'Must be mice.' I stooped down to look under the desks, but whatever it was, it had gone. Leaving the lights on, I turned towards my door just as something behind me moved along the floor.

'That's a *big* mouse.' I bent to look again but missed it. I grabbed a heavy stapler from the nearest desk, the first weapon to hand, and walked around the office, hunting a killer rat. I checked waste-paper bins and behind cabinets, but after searching the whole floor, I gave up.

Annoyed by the day's string of distractions, I dropped into my chair and snatched back my pen. But as I stared at the desk full of papers, my appetite for them plunged. My fire had finally been extinguished, and I decided to go home.

THREE

As promised, Philip worked us all through Saturday, and most of Sunday too. Keisha stayed on my mind and I wanted to call, but in her temper, she hadn't left her parents' number. By Sunday afternoon, I needed to hear a friendly voice and took a break to call Sarah, my sister.

'You've just caught me, we're going to the carol service.' I could hear that she'd run for the phone.

'I just wanted to firm things up for next week.' I picked up my pen and twirled it in my fingers.

'Adam will pick you up from the station on Friday. Is that still the plan? Did you decide on how long you're staying?'

'You win. I'll come back after New Year.' I doodled stars on my pad.

'Really? That's brilliant!'

I wanted to go back after Boxing Day but had succumbed to Sarah's pressure to take a longer break.

'I'll need a rest before I attack my promotion.'

'You've been promoted?'

'It's imminent. I've got a new portfolio and promotion's going to follow.'

'You'll be running that place soon.'

'Hardly, but I'm trying my best.'

'You're bloody amazing.' This was the stroking I needed.

'Is David coming?' My brother was spending Christmas with his prospective in-laws but wanted to join us for New Year.

'Yes, him and Lucy. It'll be a houseful.'

'Good.'

'Honestly, I can't wait to see you, Peter. But I must go, they're waiting in the car.'

The short conversation did the trick of lifting my mood. As the eldest, Sarah had always looked out for me, whether it was beating off the bullies in the playground or deflecting Father's bullying at home. And now she kept me afloat in the grown-up world, where relationships were still no easier.

Philip finally released me at six, and by the time I walked back into work on Monday, it felt like I'd never been away. The meeting with Shelltec went well and in his usual, personal style, Philip sent his secretary over with a bottle of champagne to thank me. I invited Keisha round on Tuesday to drink.

Keisha arrived with an air of the unforgiving. She marched into the living room with hardly a hello and tossed her coat onto the chair. She looked amazing in her tight, long-sleeved scarlet dress, her brown eyes blazing with sexiness. I leant in and caught her cheek with a kiss aimed for her mouth.

'You look lovely,' I said.

'Thanks. I've brought this.' She held a bottle of red wine between us, her long, painted nails matching her dress.

I took the bottle and we walked out to the kitchen. I put the wine on the counter and opened the fridge.

'Fancy a bit of this?' I presented the chilled Dom Pérignon.

'I can't drink that tonight, I'll be wrecked. I'm presenting to the governors tomorrow.' Keisha was head of communications for a private school in Chelsea. 'Let's save it and have some wine.'

I raked through the drawer for the corkscrew and pulled the wine open with a satisfying pop. I reached for glasses, poured out two modest measures and passed one to Keisha.

'Cheers,' I said.

'He might be a control freak, but he isn't cheap.' She admired the vintage Champagne's label.

'No, he can afford it.'

'Yes, he can definitely afford to buy you.'

'Oo, that's harsh.'

She shrugged her shoulders in response and carried her glass to the lounge. I followed and we sat on the two-seater sofa, the flat cushions providing little protection against its sharp springs. I brushed her hand with my fingers, but she hadn't yet thawed.

'I'm sorry for getting angry with you. I thought you understood that it was an important weekend. Everyone was there. I wanted you to meet them.'

'I did understand. It's just that Philip—'

'Owns you?'

'No, not at all.'

'So, you wanted to stay then.'

I couldn't win this. 'No... okay. He does own me in a way. Sometimes, I just have to do what he asks.'

'Hmm... well, let's forget it.' She relaxed a little and picked up my hand. 'It's gone now, and there's always Christmas.'

'Christmas?' I shifted in my seat.

'You'll meet some of them then.'

'I'm sure I told you that I'm going to my sister's.'

'Going to your sister's?' She dropped my hand and sat forward, her eyes fired with fury.

'Why don't you come to Sarah's? I know she'd love to meet you.'

'Yes, I was obviously the first person on your mind when you made that plan.'

'It wasn't like that—'

'Mum's looking forward to seeing us. Why don't you ring Sarah and rearrange?'

'I can't.' No sane person ever cancelled on Sarah.

'I don't believe this.' She sat back in silence, arms folded and staring at the wall.

'Keisha—'

'Look, I've got an important day tomorrow and I need an early night. I probably should go.'

'Really? You've only just got here.'

'I know. I shouldn't have come.' She stood and wrapped her coat around her.

'Don't be like that. It's a misunderstanding, that's all.'

'Something doesn't feel right.'

'What do you mean?'

'I can't explain it. It's just a feeling I've had all day. Look, I'm sure I'll feel better tomorrow. Let's talk then, okay?'

I rose and, knowing I was beaten, gave her a peck goodbye.

I called Keisha several times the next day, but every time her assistant answered, and Keisha never called back. We eventually spoke on Thursday, snatching a few words before her meeting. She itched to get off the phone and I forgot to ask for her number to call over Christmas.

That evening I got home shattered, just after eight, and still had to pack for Sarah's. I'd bought her a sentimental Christmas card, with 'special love' from her brother, and hunted on the coffee table for a pen. I tossed around the papers and magazines and knocked something onto the floor. I looked and saw the hardback book. It lay on the carpet with the business card staring up. I crouched and reached out to take it, and baulked at those grisly words: '*Find me in death – bye, bye.*'

I turned the card over to the name and wondered about Mr Featherstone.

Then a knock at the door made me jump. I hauled myself up to answer.

'Hi. I hope I didn't disturb you.' Isha, my neighbour, stood in her coat.

'No, not at all.'

'I wanted to give you this.' She handed over a Christmas card.

'Thank you.' I didn't have one for her and felt embarrassed. 'I'm a bit rubbish at these things.'

'That's fine, I wasn't expecting one back. Did you say you're going away?'

'Yes, tomorrow. Sorry, do you want to come in for a drink?'

'No, it's okay, I'm on my way out. I just wanted to catch you to say have a good Christmas.'

'Thanks, that's really nice.'

I walked back into the lounge and stopped in my tracks. The book was now on the table.

'I don't remember picking you up.' But I was knackered, so anything was possible. However, what bothered me more was the pen lying in plain sight next to it. I picked up the biro and stared at it. 'Okay, I'm going crazy.' Shaking my head to throw off mad thoughts, I resumed my efforts to pack.

FOUR

I woke December 23rd to find a frost gleaming in the morning dark, turning the pavements into ribbons of sparkling diamonds. I lugged my canvas holdall to the office, planning a quick getaway to the train. Of course, I knew Philip would have other plans. Around two he caught me talking to Ajay and came over.

'Peter.' My heart sank. 'If you're going to take so much time off, I'll need a run down on your accounts.'

'Yes, Ajay's pulling that together.' I winked at Ajay – we were ahead of him.

'Great, both of you, three-thirty in my office. I'm cracking open a twenty-year-old malt.' He rubbed his tanned hands together.

He knew I had plans. 'Sorry, Philip, I can't. I'm catching a train in an hour.'

'Oh, right.' He turned to Ajay. 'I'll see you later then.' Philip stomped back to his office.

'Don't worry, mate.' Ajay patted my arm. 'I've got it sorted. He'd have you here twenty-four seven if he could.'

I had strong back-up in Ajay. Not only would he cover my accounts; he'd watch over the team and be generous with leads. This wasn't selflessness, of course; he was biding his time before challenging for my crown. For now, it made sense to embrace him and reap the rewards.

I flagged a taxi to Liverpool Street and, in a fight with the tide of Christmas travellers, regretted skimping on a first-class ticket. I looked over at the busy ticket office and considered changing it when an echoey voice bounced through the lofty ceiling and announced that my train was at platform eight. Taking no chances, I made for the gate.

An inspector waved me through without checking my ticket, losing his grip on the swell. I passed two grimy carriages before reaching coach 'E' and climbed up inside, glad to be out of the station draughts and diesel stink. I found my reserved seat and plonked down next to the window, hoping to keep the aisle seat free. But I was soon trapped by an overweight, middle-aged man in a stained, cheap and shiny black suit. He claimed the arm rest between us before I thought of it and set down four cans of lager on his pull-down table. Without waiting for the journey to start, he cracked one open, the sour smell invading my air. Thankfully, I'd picked up a paper, and avoiding any chance of conversation, buried myself in the news. Cursing my first-class stinginess, I weathered the first throb of a headache.

The train lurched into action and the station's dirty glow gave way to the London sky. The bright, bitter day spawned veins of purple cloud, gradually deepening into blue as dusk spread.

I turned my head as my neighbour snapped open another can and resented his sprawled-out comfort. I squeezed into a new position, relieving my squashed legs, and then turned back to the window. Shops, offices and high-rise flats passed, until eventually, they gave way to playgrounds, parks and then fields. And soon, Philip felt a country away, thoughts of work gave way to daydreaming, and I settled into my escape.

At Ipswich, my tormentor alighted, allowing me to unfold and spread. We pulled out of the station into a dark December world, the windows reflecting the inside of the train instead of the view of the countryside. I'd done as much as I could of the crossword and, tossing the paper aside, closed my eyes.

The train's rhythm rocked me into a doze, but my neck angled awkward against the seat rest and stopped any nodding off. A jumble of thoughts bobbled through. I wondered how Ajay had fared with Philip. Then I drifted to Keisha and wished that we'd parted on better terms. I planned to make it up to her in the New Year; I'd take her somewhere extravagant and pamper her. And we would make that trip to see her parents. And then I thought about this first Christmas without Mum, and drifted, lost, missing her.

I must have fallen asleep because I opened my eyes to see Norwich station. Caught out and confused by the sudden end to the journey, I threw together my things and rushed to the door.

A flurry of people poured out of the train, but the station was quiet compared to Liverpool Street. I followed the flow down to the exit and couldn't miss my brother-in-law's massive frame, his burly body sculpted by a lifetime of farming.

Adam reached to shake my hand. 'Did you have a good journey?' My soft office hands met his honest, calloused skin.

'Yes, thanks, no delays for a change.'

'You're bang on time, I've only just parked.'

I followed his wide stride out of the station into a breezy, rainy spray. I dipped my head for cover, but Adam walked tall, regardless. We dodged through cars and taxis and reached his parked Land Rover. Adam lifted my bag and swung it onto the bench seat ahead of me. I climbed up and was still brushing mud from the leather when Adam fired the engine and pulled off.

'Looks like we're going to hit traffic.' Adam nodded ahead.

'Maybe there's been an accident.'

'I think it's a mixture of rush hour, Christmas shoppers and the rain.'

Sure enough, we joined a tailback and then crawled along the choked road. The windscreen became a misted curtain, the blowers making little impact.

'I can't see a thing.' Adam leaned forward to rub a hole with his hand. I wiped the side window with my coat arm, to stare out onto people scurrying along the greasy pavement, their coats clasped against the rain.

'Could be worse, could be snowing,' I said.

'The boys would be happy with that.'

We eventually left the town lights and drove into back roads as black as coal. The truck's main beam cut through to illuminate corners and hedges that Adam negotiated at uncomfortable speed. We talked about the weather in London, the jobs to do around the farm during the winter and the benefits of not keeping animals. However, Adam was not much of a talker, and without awkwardness, the conversation dried into silence.

In daylight I might have had a chance, but I was lost until a cluster of houses pierced the night and a sign announced our entry into Lower Tursham. The warm, yellow-lit windows of the farmhouse glowed ahead and my whole body sighed, releasing the city-life stresses.

Then Adam swerved, almost veering off the road. 'A bloody cat! I think I missed it.' By the guilt in his voice, I wasn't so sure and banished the image of a lonely, old lady, waiting for her cat to come home for Christmas. I hoped Adam was right.

We turned onto the farm lane and slowed to absorb potholes before rolling onto the wide, gravel drive. Adam jumped out and grabbed my bag, and I followed, crunching up to the house and then through the back door. Warmth rushed out of the kitchen into my face, bringing a smell of meat and frying onions. A dog gave a rough bark, and two boys squealed as they jumped and clung onto Adam.

'Hello!' Sarah wrapped her arms around my neck before I could close the door.

'Hello,' I echoed. 'Hi, Michael. Hi, Andrew.'

'Hello, Uncle Peter.' They giggled and chased Chester, their golden retriever, as he brushed around my legs and left blond hairs on my jeans. I'd wisely left my suit hanging safely in the office.

'The kettle's on. You must be dying for a cuppa,' said Sarah.

'Yes, please.' I peeled off my coat, passing it into Sarah's waiting hand. She looked well, her blue, Tyler eyes bright and smiley. She'd tied her platinum hair into an untidy ponytail and hidden her slim figure under a navy, cable-knit jumper.

'Boys, let me get changed.' Adam strode into the hall with a boy on each leg. 'Wrestle with Uncle Peter.'

'They never leave him alone,' said Sarah. 'He loves it.'

The kitchen was the most used room, a coming-together space in a mix of eras, documenting something from each family that had served it. A six-foot oak table, marked by a century of food preparation and feasting, sat altar-like in the centre. Eight high-back, spindled, wooden chairs crowded around it, facing in like chatting friends. Despite the table's size, there was ample space for a tired, beige Aga and the contrasting modern fridge and front-loading washing machine. A tall dresser almost looked the part with its arranged dinner-service display, but books, toys, cards, and empty jars overran its shelves. And above us, shining copper pans hung from a ceiling rack, polished and never to be used.

Half-done jobs filled every corner. Dirty mixing bowls waited in the porcelain sink to be washed and a basket of clothes sat on the tiled floor. On the worktop, round, golden biscuits rested, cooling on a rack, next to a plate of snow-dusted mince pies. It all spoke of comfort, homely things and safe family life. Whoever Sarah was, she wasn't her mother's daughter. Mum's kitchen was neater than a drill sergeant's mess and cleaned within an inch of its life. And had it not been, my father would've popped.

Sarah filled three non-matching mugs with tea and brought them over. We pulled out chairs and sat.

'Something smells good.' My starved stomach hankered after the cooking meat.

'It's beef stew. Is that okay?'

'Sounds great.'

'Adam, your tea's ready,' Sarah called. I could hear the kids squealing upstairs; he still hadn't escaped. 'So, what've you been up to?'

'Oh, work, and more work mainly.'

'What about Keisha?'

'I'm in her bad books. She wanted me to spend Christmas with her.'

'What? You hardly know her.'

'That's what I assumed. But apparently not.'

'Well, tough, it's my turn.'

'It's just been difficult. I've let her down a couple of times and she was already pissed off with me. But work is really critical now, with the promotion.'

'Mum would be so proud of you.' The unexpected reminder of my loss bit harder than expected. This Christmas without her would be a trial. Then Sarah added, 'And Dad, of course.' I didn't challenge the lie. Mum's over-attention to my needs had fuelled my father's dislike. But it was *his* approval I prayed for, desperate to do something he'd notice and praise. And back with Sarah, I could remember those days of being a mistake, an unwanted third, upsetting the balance and, as he'd say, always spoiling things. I tried my best to prove him wrong, but when Mum died of the weakened heart that I'd gifted her at my birth, I finally accepted that I meant nothing. There was something else too – a deep, dark feeling that I couldn't quite catch…

'Where've you gone?' Sarah peered at me.

'Just… remembering.'

'Oh, Peter, I'm so glad you're here.' She stood and flung her arms around me again, and in the surprise of being claimed, I swallowed the lump of a tear.

'I know, it's just hard to get the time—'

'Well, you're here now and I'm going to make the most of you!'

Another cup of tea and four home-baked ginger biscuits later, I carted my bag to the bedroom. The farmhouse had been built in the 1800s, and with its uneven floorboards and sloping doorframes, it lived up to the part.

Walking into the guest room, the warmth of the family home felt a world away. Yellowing wallpaper and bare, paint-spattered floorboards cried out for care. A draught blew through the crumbling window frame and thin curtains swayed in the breeze. With a nod to comfort, a plump, flowery eiderdown lay on the double bed and a tatty, sheepskin rug covered a patch of floor. The varnished oak furniture – a bookshelf, chest of drawers, bedside table and a chair – were old, but not old enough to look classy.

I threw my holdall onto the bed, and it sank lopsidedly into the springs. I unpeeled the zip and at first wasn't sure what I saw. The pieces drifted together in my mind. It was the stolen book. I stood, struggling to remember packing it, when a knock diverted my attention.

'Is the room okay?' asked Sarah.

'Yes, perfect.'

'It gets chilly in here, so if you need a heater, let me know. Red or white?'

'Eh? Oh, either. Both. Seriously, I'm happy to go with the flow.'

'Ha! Literally. See you in a min.'

I picked up the book. In the cold room, its title, *The Silent Accusation*, felt spiteful. I sensed it biding its time, waiting to spill secrets and orchestrate revenge. Amused by my drama, I dropped it onto the bedside table and started to unpack. My clothes fitted inside two of the chest's drawers, and after arranging my aftershave and other bits on top, I joined everyone downstairs.

After dinner, the kids sloped away to watch television and I collected the plates.

'No, leave it. I'll do that.' Sarah rose from the table.

'You'd better do what she says,' Adam warned with a wink. 'More wine?'

'Of course,' I said after Adam had already started glugging out a glassful of full-bodied red. 'You've got a great place here.'

'Yes, we like it,' Sarah said as she put her arm around Adam.

Adam said, 'I've lived here all my life. Can't say I like it – it's just home. Couldn't imagine being anywhere else, really.'

'Hmmm. Must be good to really belong somewhere.'

'Ah, baby brother, you can belong with us.' Sarah shifted over to cuddle me, and I looked down to hide my eyes as emotions caught me out again. I breathed in her soapy perfume and felt her warm breath as it whispered through my hair.

'Fancy a game of cards?' Adam cut the moment.

'You know, I'm knackered. Any chance I could have a bath and go to bed? Would you mind?'

'No, of course not.' Sarah straightened up. 'I'll go and run it for you.'

Adam poured out the rest of the wine and I took my glass up with me. Like the rest of upstairs, the narrow bathroom was bare and draughty. A fluffy, pink bathmat covered little of the floorboards, offering scant protection against winter. A toilet with an overhead pull-flush sat next to a sink with brass taps, and a deep, lime-scaled bath lay under the window. Taking off my clothes felt painful, but Sarah had filled the bath full of kids' bubbles, and as I eased myself in against the heat, the water embraced me like a magic healing cloak.

Laying back, the tension ebbed away, dissolving into the water. My lungs filled with the scented steam and, with a long breath out, my emotions released. Mum, Sarah, belonging, they all hit me at once, and feelings that I thought were under control all came tumbling out. Before the tears fell, I snatched the soap and scrubbed.

FIVE

I opened my eyes, disorientated by unfamiliar surroundings. Through the floor, I could hear Adam stoking the fire, the metal clang of the poker ringing loudly against the grate. My body lay cocooned in a warm nest of bedding, but I could feel the chilly room fighting its way in. I psyched myself up and opened the covers. Yesterday's clothes were piled on the chair, so I threw them on, ignoring their freezing assault on my skin. I went downstairs to find the boys and Sarah at the kitchen table.

'Morning.' Sarah poured tea. 'Did I hear you up in the night? Were you alright? Andrew, pass the milk, please.'

'No, I slept like a log. Best I've slept for weeks,' I said.

'Oh, right. Wonder what I heard. Michael! I've told you not to feed Chester at the table.' Michael put his hands over his mouth and giggled. 'I can see you, I'm not blind.'

Adam walked into the kitchen. 'Morning. Are you up for some hard work today, Peter?'

'Sure.'

'Actually,' Sarah interrupted, 'I want you to help me with a couple of things.'

'Fine by me.'

'I thought you could take Chester for a walk with the boys. And if you could find some decent holly for the table, that'd be great.'

Andrew said, 'I'm going to mend fences with Dad.'

'No, you're not, young man, you can help Uncle Peter. Adam, pass me a plate, love.'

I soon understood why Sarah wanted the boys out of her way. Like freed wild animals, they scaled trees and steep banks, while I struggled on, hiding being out of breath.

My youngest nephew, Michael, saw me as an opportunity, an audience for his show-off antics. 'Uncle Peter, watch this.' If I missed his heroic two-foot jump off a log, or his herculean throw of a stick, the feat had to be repeated. With his chestnut hair and bluey-grey eyes, he looked the image of me as a boy. However, that's where the similarity ended, because at five years old, he was already determined and feisty, where I'd been shy and unsure.

Andrew was strongminded too, but with a quiet temperament. He confidently assumed the role of expedition leader, setting quests for his brother to copy. It would take more than an old, unfit uncle to impress him. He ignored Michael's showing-off and went to do the work of bigger boys by himself.

We returned to the farmhouse with almost a whole bush of holly and armfuls of pricks and scratches. Champion Michael held up his bunch, waiting for Sarah's approval, and I found myself doing the same.

I spent the rest of the day completing tasks for Sarah, with Michael stuck to my side. We finished decorating the kitchen, tidied the toys in the lounge, filled the coal pails and fetched whatever Sarah wanted. The radio played all afternoon and Adam danced with Sarah to 'You Can't Hurry Love' until the boys jumped between them. The song got caught in my head, haunting me for the rest of the day, driving me nuts.

After dinner, we prepared the lounge for Santa in the glow of the inglenook fire. Sarah had done the room proud. A six-foot tree stood in the corner, decorated to death with multicoloured baubles and ribbons of tinsel. She'd covered the outdated sofa with Christmas patchwork blankets, their bright reds, greens and whites transforming the drab brown. Homemade garlands of dried fruit, fir cones and winter foliage hung around the room, creating a fresh spruce of Christmas with their pine and cinnamon scents.

The boys sipped warm milk from beakers and Adam helped them pin up their stockings by the fire. Their brotherly harmony was short lived and spilled into an argument over the best place to leave Santa's mince pie.

'That's enough of that.' Sarah walked in with two red hot-water bottles. 'Time for bed.' The boys groaned. 'You need to be fast asleep before Father Christmas comes, or he won't you leave any presents.' Sarah fell back on the age-old threat and sounded just like Mum.

'In a minute,' Andrew said as he moved the plate and mince pie back into the middle of the hearth.

'No, upstairs now. Come on!' Sarah looked exhausted and I didn't envy her endless catalogue of jobs. She left, knowing they would follow.

'Alright, give me a hug.' Adam pulled both boys towards him. 'Make sure you're asleep before Santa comes or you'll be on that naughty list.' I watched him squash them up in his thick arms and snuggle their necks. They erupted into giggles and a part of me tugged for something I'd never have. Then Adam growled like a bear and the boys shrieked as he chased them out of the room.

'Adam! That isn't helping,' Sarah shouted from upstairs.

When the boys were fast asleep Adam filled their stockings with presents until Sarah took over and arranged them with more artistic flair. We shared a nightcap of port and, feeling comfortably worn out, I followed them both to bed.

The boys' laughing woke me, and with a squint at the clock, I saw it was ten to six. I couldn't complain too much as I'd had nearly nine hours of sleep. I fished out jeans and a sweatshirt and heard Adam's footsteps as he walked to the bathroom. He'd just beaten me to it, and rather than wait, I made my way to the ground-floor loo. But then Adam walked out of the kitchen.

'Happy Christmas!' he said through a mouthful of mince pie.

'Happy Christmas… didn't I just hear you in the bathroom?'

'No, not guilty.' He walked into the lounge.

From behind, Sarah said, 'Sounds travel strangely in old houses,' and I turned and wished her Merry Christmas with a kiss on the cheek.

In the lounge, the boys wrestled presents out of the filled stockings. Andrew had already unwrapped a pile and Michael was ripping paper off a racing car.

'Happy Christmas,' I said.

Michael ran towards me with his prize. 'Look what Santa brought me.'

'Brilliant! I can't wait to play with that.'

Adam carried in a tray of coffee, and we sat and joined the boys to open presents. Sarah sorted through the ones under the tree.

'I'll need to tell you whose is whose from me,' I said. 'I didn't have any tags.'

31

'Well, I know that this is for you.' Sarah handed me a squidgy parcel. I tore it open to find a long, red scarf. 'I knitted it myself.'

'Thank you, it's great.' I hoped my face looked convincing.

'You can wear it to church.' Sarah had adopted Adam's faith, or rather his church-going sense of duty.

'Church? I don't think so.'

'Oh, come on, you might enjoy yourself. Anyway, what are you going to do here on your own?'

'Watch TV?'

Adam said, 'We'll have to take your car then.'

And so, it was decided.

The medieval church stood at the heart of the village, its square tower more castle-like than godly. Inside, dancing candles lit musty, crumbling walls and wooden pews cracked as they filled with high-spirited families, dressed in their Christmas best. Adam stood in a ring of men, talking business not Jesus. I saw no invite to join them and settled with Sarah's procession of friends and acquaintances, all of whose names I'd forgotten by the next introduction. I observed her in the foreign habitat, mingling with doctors, teachers, councillors and women from the institute, and saw the stranger she'd become.

Adam walked over to join us, but before we could speak, the organ belched, and like circus seals, everyone stood, poised to perform.

I faked my way through carols I half-recognised from school. The reverend spoke about love in that rhythm reserved for clergy, and in its see-saw flow, I switched off. But then he asked us to think about people we'd lost, and memories of Mum flooded back. *Here we go*, I thought, and bit my lip to keep control. I distracted myself by studying the stain-glass windows, trying to work out the story they told.

With the service creeping past the half-hour, the boys became fidgety. Adam controlled them with a single, hard stare, but I also noticed Sarah trying not to yawn. Then we sang one final carol, raising the roof to 'Oh Come All Ye Faithful', and it was done; we were free to go.

The way out became a bottleneck with Reverend Boyle shaking everyone's hand to bestow a 'Happy Christmas and the love of Christ'. Michael and I found ourselves in a scrum of families, and as we waited to escape, I shrugged at Sarah, who was already free. When it was our turn, the reverend stared at me, looked down to Michael and then frowned back to me. Michael skipped off towards Andrew, but the reverend took my hand and wouldn't let go.

'Are you the brother that Sarah's told me so much about?'

'I could be. I'm Peter.'

He drew me towards him and whispered, 'I feel that you carry something. I think Michael sees it too.'

'What? What do you mean?'

He gripped my hand tighter. 'This is not the place, Peter. Please, come and see me while you're here.'

'Reverend,' an old lady practically pushed me out of the way, 'you must try Mrs Jackson's pudding.' She held out a foil-wrapped bowl.

As I turned away, I saw Sarah watching. I walked over to join her.

'What was that all about?' she said.

'He thinks that I should go and see him.'

'Why?'

'He didn't really say.' She looked at me, puzzled. 'Probably knows I'm new to all this.'

'That's strange. Perhaps he's thinking of buying up shares.' She laughed.

'Well, he's a bit over the top.'

'He can be. He's harmless, though.'

'Anyway, I think I'll pass.' I smiled back at Sarah with more confidence than I felt, still unnerved by his behaviour.

We returned home, and with Christmas dinner, a walk with Chester, family games and more food, the rest of the day passed. I crashed out with Sarah to watch *Death on the Nile* but by the end of the film I was snoring.

On Boxing Day, Adam's sister Liz and her husband Terry came round with their girls. Jane and Lucy were a couple of years older than the boys, and Andrew couldn't hide his admiration, letting Jane boss him around and decide who was playing what.

In the evening we chatted and played rummy at the kitchen table, while the children watched TV. Then Michael, overtired and teary, came into the kitchen and climbed onto my knee. He pulled at my jumper sleeve. 'Uncle Peter, read me a story.'

'Okay. I'm in the middle of a game, so you'll have to wait a minute.'

'No, now!'

'Michael, don't be rude!' said Sarah. 'Uncle Peter's told you, he'll read when he's finished. But only if you're a good boy.' She turned to me. 'I think it should be a bedtime story, he's overtired.'

'I'm not tired!' Nevertheless, he slipped off my knee and ran upstairs to get ready. We finished the hand and I followed him up.

The lop-sided landing wasn't the steadiest place for a body full of alcohol. And as I made my way towards Michael's door, my drunken eyes saw something move.

'Uncle Peter?' I heard Michael say, but before I could answer, he screamed. I burst into his room, but then he screamed louder, and in a heartbeat, Sarah was there.

'What's wrong? What happened?' she asked him.

'Uncle Peter made me frightened.'

My eyes signalled to Sarah my innocence, but she stared back with a 'now look what you've done' expression, while soothing Michael and explaining that I was playing a joke. I stood, torn by what to say to make things better, watching them hug. Then, after being the mean outsider for longer than enough, I left her, reassuring him that I wouldn't do it again.

In the kitchen I re-joined the others and waited to be dealt into the game.

Adam looked across. 'What's the matter with him?'

'Something scared him.' I shrugged.

'Not that monster under his bed?'

'Adam!' Liz said, giggling, just as Sarah walked in.

'He's just dropped off,' Sarah said as she picked up her empty wine glass. 'Anyone need another drink?'

'What was wrong?' Adam asked again.

Sarah thought to glance at me but stopped herself. 'Nothing really, something spooked him.'

Adam chuckled and Liz said, 'Poor mite.'

'Yes, he's exhausted, bless him. It's best not to excite him when he gets like that.' And with that mild jab, the subject was closed. But Sarah's mood had changed enough for me to feel like I had spoiled things. There was no opportunity to defend myself and I couldn't check with Sarah why, when Michael had been expecting me, he'd been so scared.

Soon after, we finished the game, and Liz, Terry and the girls left. Feeling worn out, drunk and disproportionately annoyed, I said goodnight and went to bed.

SIX

The twenty-seventh dawned bright, but the night left a thin layer of ice on the inside of my window. Dampness clung to my clothes, and I shivered as I rushed to dress.

When I walked into the haven of the kitchen, Michael wouldn't meet my eye. Sarah passed me a plate of eggs and bacon and I helped myself to tea from the pot.

'I've got a bloody hangover,' said Sarah. 'I shouldn't have opened that last bottle. Boys, tone it down, please.' Without a hangover, their clatter was painful. 'I didn't sleep well either – I kept dreaming that someone was trying to get in.'

'I heard it too, Mummy,' said Michael.

'No, darling, it was only a dream.' She brushed his brow, smiling to reassure him.

'Our doors are thicker than Fort Knox,' said Adam. 'No one can get in. And failing that, I've got my shotgun.'

'Yeah. Bang! Bang!' Andrew shot his invisible rifle. 'Let's kill them, Dad.'

'Adam, that's a bit much,' said Sarah.

'Nonsense, what do you say, boys?'

'No, Daddy, no!' Michael's eyes bubbled with tears.

'It's okay, Michael, Daddy's only joking.' Sarah stared hard at Adam.

'Michael, don't be a baby,' said Adam.

'Yeah, *cry*-baby,' Andrew echoed.

'Don't call him that! He's still tired after last night, that's all.' Sarah rubbed Michael's head.

'No, I'm not!' The tears came streaming.

'Hey.' Adam reached for Michael. 'Come here, tiger.' Michael sobbed into Adam's chest. Sarah watched for a while and then, as if her thoughts had put something together, she looked at me. She'd remembered something, and so had I. Without letting the thought grow, she stood to shake it off, clashed the plates together and took them to the sink.

I tried to break the tension. 'I'll take the boys out with Chester.'

'No!' Sarah looked round and, realising her reaction, softened. 'They want a trip out to the village with me.'

'Okay… I'll just take Chester.'

Sarah turned back to the sink and poured hot water into the bowl. 'We'll let you get some peace from us.'

There was nothing to say to that, so I took my plate and mug over to the sink and went to get washed and changed.

An hour later, I took Chester's lead from the back of the kitchen door and walked over to his bed by the Aga. As I tried to clip it on, he bared his teeth and pulled away. 'What's got into you?' I patted his head and he growled and bared his teeth again. 'Suit your bloody self!' I snapped, and left him to his bed.

As it turned out, Chester had the best plan because heavy rain drove me back indoors after ten minutes. With everyone out doing their own thing, the house rested, noiselessly catching its breath. I broke the dense silence by clicking on the kettle and agitating a mug, jar and spoon to make coffee. As I waited for the water to boil, my thoughts strayed to Philip. He'd be missing me by now. I thought about him pacing, impatient for my return.

I stirred my coffee and looked out of the window at the bouncing rain and wished I'd brought some work. I'd not planned for amusing myself and had only packed clothes. Then something clicked, and I remembered, there was something else too. I finished drinking my coffee and went to fetch the book.

Stepping onto the landing, something felt wrong. I felt super-aware, as if, just at that moment, time had frozen. I saw everything in minute detail, my skin sensing every atom of air. I looked again for the shadows by Michael's door, and in that state, I saw them. A fleeting figure dissolved as I focused my eyes.

I stopped still, waiting, and when it seemed safe, I took a step. And then another. And then… clang! The hall-clock chime sent my heart through my chest.

'For fuck's sake!' I burst out laughing in relief. It was the house's creaks and shadows playing on my nerves. I strode towards my bedroom and threw open the door. The book was still on the bedside table, and I snatched it and retreated downstairs.

In the lounge, the fire was low and, pretending to know what to do, I poked it a bit and chucked on a shovel of coal. Black smoke bellowed out, streaming up into the chimney. Unimpressed at my skills, I left it to itself and made myself comfortable in Adam's armchair.

I turned my attention to the book and opened it at the business card. Reunited with my eerie-messaged friend, I tucked the card into the back pages, out of my eyeline, and flipped to chapter one.

My enthusiasm waned with the long-winded sentences that took military endurance to follow. I read about Jacob Coates, accountant and part-time author from 1900s Brighton. When his wife confronted him about his affair, he snapped and stabbed her to death. Panicked, he buried her in the cellar and claimed that she'd walked out to start a new life with *her* lover. Strangely stimulated by his crime, Jacob wrote about it, capturing it in gruesome detail for a future novel. As a precaution, he hid the incriminating notebook in the bracket under his desk.

What a stupid thing to do, I thought. I flipped the page and jumped at Sarah staring at me.

'Shit, I didn't hear you come in.'

'You were miles away. Do you want tea?'

'It's okay, I'll make it.' I wedged the business card into the chapter and went to give Sarah a hand.

The house came alive with activity, and after the break from me, Michael seemed better. We played with his building bricks, making a tower and then smashing it down. I thought he'd forgotten our misunderstanding, but at bedtime he asked Adam to read him a story with a purpose in his voice that stung.

I called it a night just after ten with the intention of finishing the book. In my cold sheets I found the police searching for the missing woman, but after questioning Jacob and finding no evidence, the case was dropped. Jacob made a fresh start in London, selling his Brighton house and auctioning off his furniture. Of course, he forgot to retrieve his notebook and the desk's new owners found it and handed it to the police. Jacob was arrested, tried and hanged.

I closed the book, disappointed with the story. I'd been foolishly hoping for something interesting and credible, and some meaning as to why the book seemed to be stalking me.

I clicked off the lamp, settled into the cosy sheets but annoyingly felt the urge to pee. I wrestled with it, wondering if I'd last 'til morning, but I had to give in and go.

The warmth of bed evaporated into the chilly air, and when my feet reached the end of the rug, they touched cold, hard floorboards. An arctic draught streamed under the bedroom door and licked at my ankles. And then I heard a noise. I paused, listening. It was an odd sighing, a raspy rise and fall. I realised it was Adam's snoring. Reassured, I opened the door and hurried into the bathroom.

In the night quiet, the flush crashed like waves, and I dropped down the seat lid to dampen it. Moving on to wet my hands, the sighing sound rose above the dying flush. *What a funny snore*, I thought, as I swung open the bathroom door and came face to face with Adam. I yelped like I'd trapped my paw.

'Sorry, didn't mean to scare you.' He brushed past me into the bathroom.

I returned to my room, jumped into bed and wondered what it was that I'd heard. *Sounds travel strangely in old houses*, I remembered, but somehow, that made me feel worse.

SEVEN

The novelty of relaxation was long gone and my itch for the office grew stronger. I pushed the urge out of my waking mind, only to see it haunt me in dreams, where Philip interchanged with my father.

Michael's trust in me grew and although he let me read his bedtime stories, we always did that downstairs. Sarah still hadn't tired of me, but we slipped into 'big sister, little brother', putting me on a par with the kids. By New Year's Eve, I was craving Lucy and David's company.

Everybody loved David. He had the golden hair of the gods and a body to match. He'd inherited every notable Tyler trait – self-importance, arrogance, vanity, pride. With the emotional and financial sponsorship of my father behind him, success cascaded, propelling him to partner in the family law firm before the age of thirty. If he fell into a sewer, he'd find Atlantis. He met Lucy when she joined the firm as a trainee solicitor, and it took him the best part of five minutes to ask her out. After being an item for three years, they were now planning their September wedding.

Michael and Andrew tested Sarah's nerves with their constant asking about when Uncle David was coming. To give her peace, I took them on a walk to the village. The boys were used to making the journey by car and complained all the way about the distance. I bribed them both with the promise of sweets and Andrew pushed for a comic. When we reached the village shop, I let them both choose a comic and then Andrew demanded a can of Coke, and had the cheek to sulk when I said no.

We returned home and huddled around the Aga to warm our hands, while Sarah made hot chocolate. Andrew showed Sarah his Spider-man comic and, not wanting to be outdone, Michael pushed his way in to steal the attention. Used to it, Andrew sat down at the table and read to himself.

'That's a very grown-up comic, young man.' I saw Sarah looking at the dark figures on the cover of Michael's *Warrior* magazine. It hadn't occurred to me to censor his choices.

'No, it's not!' Michael pulled away and went out to the hall.

'Where are you going? Uncle David will be here soon,' said Sarah.

'I'm going to my bedroom to show my friend.'

I said, 'Tell your invisible friend that you can't see him right now.'

'Stop encouraging him!'

The force of Sarah's voice stung. 'I'm not… it's only a joke…'

'He's strange enough!' she snapped.

Like you, is what she thought, but before I could respond, Adam walked in with David.

'Happy New Year!' David bellowed.

'Happy New Year.' Sarah stretched up to hug him.

'You get more gorgeous every day, sis.'

'Ah, you're such a smoothie.'

Then it was my turn for his attention. 'Fuck me! How did they get you here? Did they pay you?'

'David!' Sarah laughed.

'Good to see you too, dickhead,' I said, but David turned away before I finished planting a playful punch on his arm.

'Andrew, you're almost as handsome as me.' Despite himself, Andrew swelled.

Adam shouted into the hallway, 'Michael, Uncle David's here.'

'Where's Lucy?' Sarah was missing her one female ally.

'She's got the flu.'

'Oh no! That's awful.'

'Yep. She's really pissed off about it. Sorry, but you'll just have to put up with me.'

'Send her my love when you call her.' Sarah moved towards the kettle. 'I better make some tea.'

'Nah, I've brought this.' David produced a bottle of Moët.

Sarah raised her eyebrows. 'What, already?'

'Don't be ridiculous, it'll need to chill for at least ten minutes. We'll start with this.' David presented a bottle of Glenfiddich. Sarah shook her head but still reached for the tumblers.

It didn't take long for me to become the usual outsider. I tried to get into the conversation, but with their shared jokes about Dad and reminiscences of a family life that didn't exist for me, it was their own private club. I watched them both, swapping stories of their grown-up worlds, and a couple of times I chipped in, but they both talked over me. Adam wasn't part of it either, but he didn't count. He was content to drink and listen, while they left me to play with the other children.

As a result, I stayed up too long, keeping David to myself on New Year's night, after Adam and Sarah had gone to bed. I topped up both our glasses to make sure he didn't escape.

'I'm getting promoted,' I said.

'That's great. Pass those crisps over, will you?'

'I already manage a shitload, and—'

'Are you still thinking of moving?'

'What? Oh, you mean the flat. No... well... at some point. I can afford something better, it's just—'

'We're looking for a house for after we're married. She wants kids straight away.' He stretched out his chest and slapped me on the back, 'I'll need to replenish the Tyler stock, old boy.'

'There's Michael and Andrew.'

'They're not Tylers.' No name, no fame. 'I'm thinking of something back home in Richmond, or maybe a bit further out...' David talked on and on, and I waited for a gap that never came. Getting more and more pissed off, I drank down my whisky, filled my glass with the dregs and looked up to find him staring at me. He leaned in, about to tell a secret, but then the lights flickered off and stopped him in his tracks. In a moment, they blinked back on.

'Must be windy out there,' said David.

'It's windy in here.' I lifted my bum cheek and farted in David's direction.

'Wonderful! Well, on that note, I'm going to bed. Goodnight, darling.' He pushed his chair from the table with an ear-piercing scrape. I got up too and followed him into the hall. David was sleeping on a camp bed in the lounge, and just as we neared the door, the hall light went out, throwing us into pitch black.

Then someone ran up the stairs.

'Who's that?' I called as David tried the light switch.

Someone sighed above us and then a door opened and closed.

'What the hell… Did you hear that?' I whispered.

'I'm not deaf.'

I moved to the foot of the stairs. 'Hello?' After a few seconds, I started climbing. When my foot hit the fourth step, a figure loomed over. The lights flashed on to show Adam.

'Come on, gents, quiet, please.'

'Did you hear something?' I asked him.

'Of course I did. So did the whole village. Keep it down or you'll wake the boys.'

'It wasn't you?'

'What? Come to bed, it's almost three.'

'How bloody strange.'

'Sod this,' said David. 'I'm going to bed. See you in a few hours.' He disappeared into the lounge.

I went up to my room, into icy air. Closing the door, I took a moment to breathe, adjusting to the alcohol in my bloodstream. I pulled off my jumper and fished out my pyjamas. But then I felt the hairs prickling on the back of my neck. Someone was behind me.

I swallowed and forced myself to turn, inch by inch by inch. I came face to face with no one. I listened for a moment, the draught piercing my shivering body. Everything was deathly still.

Then I saw it. The book sat open on the bedside table, the business card standing proud. I marched over and slammed it shut, the thud vibrating the air.

Definitely too much whisky, I decided, and climbed into the cold bed. The room spun and spun like a carousel, making me want to throw up. I held back the sickness, prayed I'd be fine and, at some point, passed out cold.

I woke in a sweat with a vice squeezing my head. Trying to ease it, I curled onto my side, but that just made it worse. When I looked at my watch it was nearly eight, so I gave in and got up. I staggered into the kitchen to find everyone tucking into bacon and eggs. The smell turned my stomach as I plopped myself down. Showing no signs of suffering, David passed me a coffee and I cradled it, trying not to retch.

The morning passed in a blur and when time left no choice, I shuffled to my room to pack. I emptied the chest back into my bag, most of it clean thanks to Sarah. When I turned to the bed, the book was waiting. I reached out and took it and felt its weight in my hand. There was no point in carrying it home. I tossed it on the bed, watched it slide almost over the edge and then carried my holdall to the door. As my hand touched the doorknob, my mind shared a crazy thought.

Perhaps there's a reason to take it. I looked back over my shoulder, wondering why I might need the book. *Bloody hell, just leave it.*

But it seemed to have some sort of hold on me. I managed to open the door, but with my foot on the landing I paused… *Don't leave it in Sarah's home.* That new thought surprised me, as if it hadn't been my own. Irritated but taking no chances, I walked to the bed, picked up the book and chucked it into my bag.

Back in the kitchen, David and I said our goodbyes. Michael stayed in the lounge, while Andrew stopped playing and came to shake our hands.

'Michael, come on, they're going,' Sarah shouted, and then reached to give me a hug. 'It's been so lovely having you both here.'

'Thanks for everything, I've had a really good time,' I said.

'I suppose the next family gathering will be my wedding.' David pulled a terrified face.

'Yes, but you better not leave it that long before you come back with Lucy.'

Adam picked up his keys. 'Right then, better get going.'

'Uncle Peter, I drawed this for you.' Michael ran into the kitchen and held out a felt-tip picture. 'It's you and me reading a story.'

'Thanks, mate, it's brilliant!' I squatted down to hug him. 'I'm going to put this on my wall when I get home.' I hugged him again.

'Enough of that, you'll miss your train,' Sarah cut in. 'Adam already drives like a maniac, he doesn't need an excuse.'

'Come on, boys, let's see if I can do it in fifteen.' Adam winked at Sarah and walked out. I picked up my bag and followed with David, while Sarah came and waited on the doorstep.

The three of us climbed into the Land Rover, squeezing onto its bench seat. David had let me get in first, making sure he had the window. He stretched his legs apart, pushing me onto the gearstick. With final waves goodbye we set off down the drive.

A curtain of fog forced Adam to crawl to the road, but there the air thinned and we gathered speed. Potholes played havoc with my hangover but, alone with the two of them, I needed something off my mind.

'What was all that about last night?' I said.

'What?' said David.

'The strange stuff when we went to bed.'

'It was you two clowns. You're lucky Sarah didn't hear you,' said Adam.

'No, the lights went out, and then we heard someone going up the stairs.'

Adam laughed. 'What the hell were you drinking?'

'He's good at hearing things,' said David. 'He used to scare the shit out of Sarah.'

'David, you heard it too.'

'Don't be an idiot.' David leant forward and switched on the radio. 'You don't mind, do you, Adam?'

'No, I like it.'

'Good, I'm too knackered to talk.'

Silenced as usual, I stared at the road, wishing I was already home.

EIGHT

Monday 3rd January was a velvet-black morning, more akin to midnight than dawn. The streets to Angel tube still slept, but at Bank, early workers scurried without words and dispersed into the crowd of city buildings – offices and no shops, monumental constructions that hid away the heartbeat of the city.

At Montgomery's, I bounded past the security guard and caught the lift to the fifth floor. Philip had beaten me in.

'Happy New Year! Did you have a good break?' he said.

'Yes, thank you, really good. You?'

'You look well on it.'

'I feel it. Can't wait to get stuck in.'

'Perfect. Oh, and by the way, while you were away Donald Shields dropped in.' Philip never wasted time when getting to the point – Donald was one of my new clients.

'Is everything okay?'

'Yes, fine, he just wanted to go over a couple of things. He's keen to weigh you up. Why don't you call and offer him lunch?'

'Of course, will do.' Like the professional ball-breaker he was, Philip was in excellent form.

The morning team meeting was high-spirited, a reunion of like-minded souls. Helen had snatched a major account from under a competitor's nose. Ajay had batted off everything from Philip and mined three new leads that looked promising. He dropped the word bonus several times, as always living in hope. I then met with the analysts before launching into trading and working solidly until noon.

Taking a break to stretch my legs, I remembered to call Keisha. With no phone at home, ringing her on Sunday had been a pain, and after three fruitless treks to the phone box, I'd given up. I was half expecting the brush-off from her assistant when Keisha picked up the phone.

'Hi, Peter.'

'I'm so pleased I've caught you, I wasn't sure when to call.'

'Did you have a good Christmas?'

'Yes, thank you.'

'Thanks for the necklace, it's lovely.' I'd bought her a gold chain – sophisticated, expensive and, more to the point, safe.

'I'm glad you liked it. And thanks for the cufflinks, I'm wearing them now. The sapphires go well with my suit.'

'Blue's your colour.'

'Yes, seems so.' I straightened the square links. 'Do you want to come over tonight?'

'This week's tricky, with the new term.'

'Sorry, of course. What about Saturday?'

'I'm going to the cinema with Adrian.' Adrian was her friend but also her ex.

'Sunday?'

'You know… I'm not sure.'

'Oh, okay. Is it easier to call next week?'

'Peter… I've been doing a lot of thinking over Christmas—'

'Look, I'm *really* sorry about Christmas. *And* your father's birthday.'

'It's not just that... something's changed. This isn't working.'

'Let's meet up and talk about it.'

'I don't think I want that, no.'

'Come on, Keisha, don't be like that.'

'Sorry, I need to go.'

She put down the phone before I could speak. *Did she really just end it?* I sat there in disbelief. My first thought was to call her straight back, but then Ajay walked in with a client.

I tried to pour my thoughts into work but couldn't get Keisha out of my mind. I called Sarah for moral support and, as usual, she managed to shift my mood. After that I could just about concentrate and wade through the afternoon. By six I felt ready to let go of work and faced the dark journey home.

By the time I'd re-surfaced at Angel, nightfall had brought a wind that broke my resistance to the cold. I pulled up my collar and trotted along the pavement, shivering until my key turned and I stepped inside the hall.

In the lounge, I warmed up with the help of a large whisky and swapped my coat for my old, black, knitted jumper. I swiped the whisky from the sideboard and, when I poured another, saw Michael's picture on the wall. I wondered what he was up to until I realised it was way past his bedtime. After a testing day, his smile and the relaxation of Sarah's felt part of another world.

With whisky in hand, I flicked on the TV and settled on the sofa. My eyes stared blank at the picture while my mind relived losing Keisha. Before long, though, my eyes were closing. Even though it was only eight, I threw in the towel and went to bed.

At quarter-to-ten something woke me out of deep sleep. I was dropping back off when I thought I heard a knock at the door. It was too late for callers, so I knew I was mistaken, but then the knock came again.

With a mix of annoyance and disorientation, I shuffled to the door and fumbled the lock. My doorstep was empty, but something moved on the landing below.

'Hello?' I heard footsteps. 'Who's there?' Silence returned. I crept to the top stair to get a better look, but then my front door slammed and locked.

'Shit!' Then the landing light blew, plunging me into darkness.

I calmed my mind to think. Isha kept my spare key, which meant walking down the stairs, head on into danger. But I didn't have a choice.

I steadied myself and then felt my way, breath by breath, stair by stair. When I reached the solid haven of Isha's door, I pounded. After ten, long seconds, she answered.

'Peter?'

'Sorry, Isha. I know it's late, but I've locked myself out.' She stared at my pyjamas. 'The bloody bulb's just blown, it's all happening at once,' I forced a laugh. 'I think you have my spare key?'

'Yes… it's here somewhere.' She turned to a dresser and rummaged through a drawer. 'Is this one yours?' She held out a key on a yellow tab.

'Yes, thank you. You're a lifesaver!'

'Can you see alright?'

'Could you leave your door open a minute?' I ran up the stairs. I threaded the key into the Yale lock, and it turned. 'Got it, thanks, Isha.'

'You're welcome, goodnight.'

Isha closed her door and I turned to go into mine but froze. I could hear someone moving inside. Without thinking, I burst in and was met with thick darkness.

I rushed to turn on the lights and looked about. There was no sign of disturbance, and the only sound was stillness. Nothing made sense.

But then I saw it, on the floor. That bloody cursed book. I picked it up and slammed it into the sideboard, out of sight. It could stew there 'til the morning and then I would get rid.

NINE

The late-night disturbances had marred my good start to the year. On top of that, I woke with a cold. Each swallow felt like razor blades cutting my throat. With the time I'd taken off over Christmas, there was no way I could call in sick. Feeling sorry for myself, I rolled out of bed and blew my nose.

I moped around the flat getting ready, slurping strong coffee to try and clear my head. As I laced up my shoes in the lounge, I faced the sideboard and remembered the book. Its time was up. I fished it from its hiding place, stuffed it into my coat pocket and left for work.

I planned to throw it in our communal dustbin, but as I popped to the yard and opened the lid, it felt too close to home. Instead, I walked to the high street and dropped it in a bus stop bin. Part of me felt ridiculous, but my relief to be rid of it was every bit real.

When I walked into the office, my nose streamed and my head pounded. Janice, Philip's secretary, pounced on me before I'd taken off my coat.

'Sorry to bother you straight away... Goodness! You look awful.'

'It's just a cold.' I made it to my chair.

'Well, don't work too hard today.'

'I won't.'

'Sorry about this, but do you have the Feldman Holdings file? Philip said you worked on it yesterday?'

'Yes, and I put it back in the cabinet.'

'Are you sure? I've looked through it twice and can't see it.'

'Definitely.' When Janice didn't move, I sighed. 'Someone else must have it.'

'I've checked that too and no one has seen it.' Our eyes met, and she felt my frustration. 'But Eric Feldman will be here in less than half an hour and Philip needs the file.'

We went to the cabinet, and I pulled the drawer open, flicking to where it should be. There was no sign of Feldman Holdings, but a file for 'Featherstone Assets' caught my eye. In a flash, I saw the name on the business card: 'Mr E H Featherstone'. Switching back to the search, I checked the whole drawer but still had no luck. Just in case, I checked the other drawers too.

Frustrated, I stomped back to my office and emptied my desk. When that didn't work, I searched the team.

'What are you looking for?' Tim stood up, ready to help.

'I can't find the bloody Feldman file.'

'Here, let me look.' Tim shifted some papers.

'I don't think it's here.'

Ajay joined us. 'You look like shit. Go and sit down and I'll sort it – it's got to be here somewhere.'

'Thanks, mate, I really appreciate it.'

Then Philip strode past. 'It's too late now, I'll manage without it.'

'I'll come into the meet—'

'No! Don't bother,' he said without turning back. I felt my cheeks colour.

Ajay said, 'Don't worry, boss, he'll cope. Come on, I'll buy you a coffee.'

The stress made my illness worse. Eric Feldman came and went, and Philip returned to his office and slammed the door. At two-fifteen Ajay came to tell me that one of the typists had found the file.

'You'd drafted a summary,' he prompted.

'Bloody hell. Yes. I remember.'

'And Lisa put the files away overnight, and unfortunately, yours slipped inside the Bailey Featherstone file.' My head snapped up at the name and Ajay mistook my expression. 'Don't be hard on her, she feels awful.'

'It's not that…' I couldn't explain this to Ajay. 'I'll have a word with her in a minute and make sure she knows it's okay.' Ajay nodded and returned to his desk.

Around four, I took a break and went to clear the air with Philip. However, Janice intercepted, advising that he needed to leave early and was already running late. Resigned to being in his bad books, I let it go and, still feeling shocking, decided to join him in calling it a day.

With each tube stop, my cold symptoms worsened. My head swam and my throat felt raw and twice its normal size. I just wanted to get home and lie down. I went up the stairs to my flat and noticed that the landing lights were now working. Isha must have complained to the landlord.

Climbing the stairs made every muscle ache and my head throbbed like it might explode. Even the sound of my door closing jarred inside my brain, and I went straight to find paracetamol. I knew there should be some in the bathroom cabinet and found the unused bottle in the corner at the back. Just as I picked them up there was a knock, knock, knock at the door and the tablets flew out of my hand onto the tiled floor. In two minds whether to answer, I stared at the smattering of glass and pills and then winced as the knocks came again. Defeated, I went to the door.

With my hand on the catch, I heard an odd, scraping noise, like a weight being dragged up the stairs. I turned the lock and peeled open the door. My landing was lit but the staircase was dark.

'Hello?' My voice echoed out into the empty halls and after a few seconds I closed the door. As I turned back to the lounge, I stopped dead in my tracks. The scraping, dragging sound was outside again. I put my ear to the door and then… thump! A violent thud knocked me back.

'Fucking joker.' I flashed open the door.

No one was there.

Right behind me, near the coat stand, a scratching noise sounded, and as I turned to look, something touched my back from the hall. Crying out, I spun and came face to face with Isha.

'Is everything alright?' she asked.

'Yes! I mean… You made me jump.'

'Sorry, I've just walked in and thought I heard you call out.'

'Did you hear the scraping?'

'What?'

'Did you hear the noises?'

'Were you moving something?'

'No, it wasn't me.' So, she'd heard it too. 'And somebody knocked on my door.'

'I didn't see them. Are you sure you're alright? You look shaken.'

'You didn't see them?'

'No.' I was puzzling it out when she added, 'As long as you're okay, I'll leave you to it.' And with that she went back downstairs.

I walked into the lounge, my legs weak with fever and my head pounding. The room felt odd, as if something was waiting to bite me if I dared to lower my guard. I'd scared myself silly by imagining crazy things and needed to calm down. To start that off, I poured a large whisky and knocked it back. I then poured another and perched in my chair.

Then the lounge door slammed shut, sending me into paralysis.

Something was in my space.

I tried to call out, but the words stuck in my throat, like a sharp, wooden block. Something banged on the lounge door and this time the dragging sound followed. It was just on the other side, coming closer and closer and closer. To my horror, the doorknob turned. Slowly, the door opened.

'*No!*' I jumped up, ready to hurl my glass.

The door stopped, suspended half-open.

I edged towards the lobby, ready to bolt back if needed. I peered in and saw nothing but hanging coats. I opened the front door to check the landing. Still, I saw nothing.

I walked to the sideboard, refilled my glass and gulped it down. This had all started with that blasted book. There was something I had missed – some reason for this nonsense. I needed to check the book again, but of course, it was now in the bin. Ignoring how sick I was feeling, I pulled on my coat.

TEN

It was half-eight, but the dark winter sky made it feel more like ten. Rain lashed down, adding to my misery, as I tried to ignore the pain inside my bones. I turned onto the high street, saw the bus stop ahead and hoped the bin wasn't full of wet, stinking rubbish. As I reached it, what I didn't expect to see was an empty, dark hole.

'Oh, shit, it's gone.' A bus neared and I stepped back to save the driver from stopping. As he passed, he hit a puddle and an arc of rain soaked my legs. 'Fucking great.' I shook what I could off my shoes and turned home.

After drying off, I changed into pyjamas and made myself some hot milk and whisky. I sank into my armchair and warmed myself through by the fire. My nerves were broken and for a moment, I felt like crying.

'For goodness' sake, Peter, you're such a baby.'

I turned the words over in my head. *For goodness' sake, Peter, you're such a baby.* I drifted to a memory.

I take a chair in the dentist's waiting room, and he sits down, not next to me but opposite. He opens *The Times*, blocking my view of him.

'Dad?'

'Hmm?'

'Will it hurt?'

'Probably.'

'What are they going to do?'

'Pull out two teeth.'

'I mean, how?'

'With pliers, I should imagine.'

Horrified by the thought, my mind races through what that might feel like. The nearest I can get is a *Tom and Jerry* cartoon. Tom is strapped down, and Jerry pulls out all his teeth in one go, leaving them chattering along on the floor, like a set of wind-up joke-shop dentures.

'Dad, what if they get the wrong ones?'

He flicks his newspaper to show I'm disturbing him. 'Look, they won't get the wrong ones. For goodness' sake, Peter, you're such a baby.'

The nurse calls my name, and he doesn't look up. As I walk towards her, I glance at him for reassurance, but his gaze is fixed on his paper. I face the mad pliers alone.

My mind switched back, and as I drained my mug, a siren wailed through the streets. My lights flickered in sympathy with the vibration of noise, before dimming and brightening again. Then electricity crackled and the lights snuffed out, abandoning me to the dark.

Moonlight cast gruesome shadows into the room, and I knew it had begun.

My ears ringed with the thumping of blood as I leapt to the sideboard for a torch. I opened the door and the lights blinked back on.

In front of me was the book.

'Is this some twisted joke?' I lifted it out, not believing my eyes. 'How the hell did you get in there?' For a moment I questioned my sanity – had I really got rid of the book?

Yes, I had thrown it into the bus bin. Something, somehow, had brought it back.

Then I remembered the priest's words: '*You carry something with you.*' What seemed so strange at Christmas was starting to make sense. Well, they'd picked on the wrong person: it was time to fight fire with fire.

ELEVEN

I hauled my shattered body into work, the fever still sapping my energy. I worked for an hour solid until my eyes ached and my back complained. Putting down my pen, I arched in my chair and, typically, that's how Philip caught me.

'Tired already?' he said.

'Just taking a moment, I've been at it a while.'

'Have you met Donald Shields yet?'

Oh, hell. With everything else going on, he'd dropped out of my mind. 'Just firming it up.'

'Good.' He walked off, clearly beyond pleasantries.

'Oh, and by the way, Philip, do you know any priests?' I muttered after him. But that flippant remark did me no favours because then, the book stuck on my mind. I tried to push it out, but after wrestling to retrieve my concentration, I gave in and thought of my plan.

One of the typists, Sonia, collected for orphans at Christmas. She was the churchy type. But Sonia spoke at five hundred decibels, and everyone would hear my business. Then there was Elena, one of the analysts, who'd invited us to her church choir charity concert. She seemed like somebody normal, and someone who'd be discreet.

I walked over to Elena's team and saw her desk empty. I scanned around and caught her disappearing into the kitchen. She was hard to miss – a striking vision of olive skin and jet-black hair tied up tight. I grabbed my coffee mug and followed.

Elena was stirring her drink by the time I walked in. I smiled to start an exchange.

'Hi, Peter. Did you have a good Christmas?'

'Yes, thanks. Feels like an age ago now, though. Did you do anything nice?'

'We had the usual gathering at home. The typical Italian feast. I think I've put on a stone.' Her jumper dress spoke otherwise.

'Sounds good. I spent Christmas with family too. Even went to church.'

'Nice.'

'I suppose you're used to that?'

'Yes.'

I struggled with what to say next and then said a clumsy, 'Do you go a lot?' She looked at me, blank. 'Church.'

'Not really, no. I might go once a month or so, it depends.'

Here goes... 'I'll tell you why I'm asking. My mother died recently—'

'Oh, I'm sorry to hear that.'

'And I found talking to the priest really helped.' She gazed into my eyes and my stomach went funny. I instantly regretted my dishonesty.

'You should definitely talk to our priest.' She'd saved me from further perjury. 'Father Ryan is lovely.'

'I feel a bit daft, but do you think I could?'

'It's not daft at all. He'd be happy to chat. I'll give you his number.'

63

'Excellent, thanks for your help.'

'I'm touched that you've trusted me with this.'

Her sincere words made me feel worse.

True to her word, she dropped by my office with the number. I was hanging on the phone for Donald Shields, so I nodded 'thank you' as I took her note.

Not wanting to rush home to another dose of the creeps, I worked through until eight. I resisted Dan and Helen trying to drag me to the pub, and they didn't mask their disappointment. Thursday drinks were something like Wednesday drinks but always lasted longer than anyone intended and kept you feeling ill until Friday's hair of the dog. The diversion would've been welcome, but I couldn't risk mismanaging Friday.

I also wanted to call Father Ryan from the office, with no one overhearing. I plucked up the courage and dialled the number.

'Hello, Father Ryan here.' In my head, I'd expected an Irishman and was thrown by a high scouse Accent.

'Hello. My name is Peter Tyler. I got your number from Elena Raniero.'

'Oh yes, Elena.'

'She thought you'd be a good person to talk to.'

'Okay. What about?'

'I don't know how to say this. It feels a bit silly now.'

'Come on, son, I don't bite. You obviously needed to call.'

'I'm not sure if it's your sort of thing but… well… I think I'm being haunted.'

'Crikey, I wasn't expecting that.'

'Sorry, perhaps—'

'No, go ahead. I'd really like to hear it.'

I replayed finding the book, my conversation with the reverend at Christmas and then all the crazy things that had happened since. I felt reassured by the 'oh my goodness' and 'please, go on' that punctuated his listening.

'You're absolutely right to take this seriously. You're caught up in something here.'

'Why is it dragging me in?'

'That's difficult to say. These things can happen for all sorts of reasons.'

'I even got rid of the book, and somehow it made its way back.'

'It's with you now anyway.' He didn't say what 'it' was, and I didn't want to ask. 'We need to look to the Lord for help – it's the only way. The book and your home must be exorcised.'

'Really? Is that something that happens?'

'Absolutely. More than you'd ever believe.'

'And you can do that?'

'I *must* do that. You can't take any chances with this. And it must be done soon.'

'Can you come tonight?'

'The earliest I can make it is Saturday. How about if I come around nine in the morning? Can you hang on 'til then?'

'Err… yes. I think so.' I wasn't feeling so sure. 'Oh, and… do you need to tell anyone? I mean, is it confidential?'

'Apart from my camera crew, I'll be alone.'

'Well—'

'I'm just kidding you, son.'

'Ah, ha! Right.'

TWELVE

I made it to Saturday in one exhausted piece. Time crawled
to nine o'clock and I counted every second past it, until
Father Ryan arrived with a firm knock, knock, knock.
I paused with my hand on the catch, for a split second
wondering whether it could be my tormentor instead, but
when I opened the door, there he stood, a tangible body of
bone and flesh.

He leant, one hand on the wall, fighting his breath back
from climbing the stairs. His light-grey overcoat emphasised
his plump, broad, figure, and his combed-over scalp shined
with sweat.

'You must be Peter?'

'Yes, come in.'

'You never said you lived up a mountain.' He dabbed
his forehead with a hanky and followed me to the lounge.

'Sorry, I'm used to it. Please, take a seat. Would you like
a drink?'

'A cup of tea would be grand.' He ignored my offer to sit
and stood peering around the walls.

'How do you like it?'

'Milk and two sugars, please. Is it okay if I have a wander

66

through the rooms while you make it? I'd like to get a sense of what we're dealing with.'

'Go ahead.'

I left him to it, and by the time I'd come back, he was transforming the coffee table into an altar with a cloth, cross, Bible and bottle of holy water. I passed him his tea and he slurped the red-hot liquid.

'That's lovely, thanks.' He slurped again. 'I sense quite a power here.'

'Really? I don't like the sound of that.'

'Don't worry, lad, leave it to me.'

Thank God, I thought as I watched him pull on his priest robe. 'What do you think it is?'

'Something attached to the book, I imagine. Sometimes spirits attach themselves to objects and come through. It's usually if they've suffered a tragedy, or violent death. Or there could be some black magic at play here, eh?' He raised one eyebrow and I felt my eyes widen at the new avenue of danger. 'Don't worry, I've seen it all.' He winked. 'Now, I'll need to get the book ready – where is it?'

My stomach flipped at the thought of it. I walked over to the sideboard, and when I opened the door, it sat there scowling. I picked it up and as I held it towards Father Ryan, he shielded himself with his hands.

'Place it down on the cloth there. The less I handle it the better.'

Father Ryan crossed himself before completing his preparations in methodical succession. I wasn't sure whether that was due to practice or nerves.

'Yes, this book has brought it through. I can feel the power in it.' He nodded to emphasise his words. 'I'm going to bless the rooms with holy water. If you could remain quiet throughout, no matter what you hear *or* see.' I nodded. 'I'll ask you to join me in prayer. I'll make it obvious when you're to do that. And then I'll exorcise the book. The whole thing should be over before you know it, unless we have a bad turn.'

'Does that happen?'

'It can do. But there's no reason to think it will today, so let's be positive. We don't want to feed it any negative energy. Now remember, son, no matter what, stay here and keep calm. If anything out of the ordinary happens, you must do exactly as I say. Is that clear?'

'Crystal.' I felt both terror and excitement.

And then he started. 'In the name of the Father, Son and Holy Ghost…' and I listened to him read scripture, appeal to the Father and demand my release from Satan in Jesus' name. He visited the other rooms, speaking incantations and spraying holy water. As promised, he asked me to kneel with him in prayer, and we blessed my soul together.

At various times he asked, 'Do you feel that, Peter?' so vehemently that I nodded even though my heathen soul sensed nothing.

At the climax, Father Ryan turned his attention to the book. He crossed it, sprayed it, damned it, sprayed it, bathed it in the love of Christ, sprayed it and crossed it again. And then he prayed in silence, before bowing his head and crossing himself one last time.

'There, Peter, can you feel that?' I had no idea what I should feel, so I erred on the side of caution and said nothing. 'The place is as still as the Sea of Galilee that the good Lord calmed himself. Amen.'

'Thank you so much, Father. It's such a relief.'

'I'm happy to take the book now. I'll destroy it. No sense in tempting fate.'

'Please do.' He picked it up and placed it in his bag.

'Can I get you more tea?'

'Oh, no, thank you. I need to be going. I have an appointment at half-past ten.'

I watched him collect his things together and when he was ready, I walked him to the door.

'It's been good to meet you, Peter, and I hope to see you at church.'

'I'll try my best,' I lied.

'Good. That's all we can hope.'

I saw him safely negotiate the stairs and then returned to the lounge. I stood for a moment to take in its mood. I walked around, breathing in the still air, savouring the peace. The place was mine again; I could feel it in my bones. It had been the strangest start to the year, but I could put it all behind me and never breathe a word.

THIRTEEN

It was a mild, pleasing day, with a keen sun that poked between the light covering of cloud. I jogged along with the constant stream of traffic, my lungs feeling the burn. At Pentonville Road, I hopped on a bus to take me to Regent's Park.

I'd craved green spaces since leaving Sarah's, but this wasn't the haven of Norfolk. Instead of countryside peace and dense greenery, bare tree branches showed the buildings beyond against a soundtrack of city hubbub. I loved the verve of the capital, but perhaps it was time to seek something else.

The park was quiet for a Saturday lunchtime, just a handful of dog walkers and people cutting through. I dodged past a young couple with a child toddling between them, and as I headed up to the boating lake, a woman caught my arm.

'Oh my goodness. Peter Tyler.'

It took a moment to recognise the face fringed by a woolly hat that almost hid her wild auburn hair. 'Anna, what a surprise. How are you?' We'd dated in the first year of university.

'I'm really good.' A broad smile spread over her face. 'Do you live around here?'

'Not far, Islington. You?'

'Just over the road in Camden. I've been here since I started at the Treasury. Where are you working?'

'Montgomery's.'

'Solicitors?'

'Heavens no. Stockbrokers.'

'Oh, really? I imagined you in the family business.'

'Yes, I turned my back on hundreds of years of Tyler tradition. But there you go. Someone has to let the side down.'

We walked and swapped stories of our lives since university. She had settled in London after doing her masters. I found out that she was single too, following the break-up of a nine-month relationship, and I wondered whether she'd be up for a friendly night out. When we reached her exit out of the park, I grabbed my chance to ask her.

'Would you like to go for dinner sometime?'

'Err…'

'No strings attached, of course.'

'Okay, yes. Why not.'

'When's good for you? I'm free most weekends.'

'I could do next Saturday, I think. Or, actually, I am free tonight.'

That was sooner than expected, but what the hell. 'Tonight's great. How about Pascal's in Covent Garden?'

'Yes, I know it. Shall I meet you there?'

'How about seven-thirty? But give me your number, just in case.'

She found a pen inside her bag and wrote her number on my bus ticket. With it tucked safely in my pocket, we went our separate ways.

Anna had been my first real girlfriend. Back then, we'd lived in each other's pockets, sleeping together in our lumpy, single beds. But my lack of commitment bothered her. I wasn't trying to be difficult; I just didn't know who I wanted to be and needed some space to find out. The final straw came when I cancelled on joining her for a weekend away, claiming my mother was ill. Her best friend caught me in a casino on a boys' night out and couldn't wait to tell Anna. I knew she hated gambling, and lying to go to a casino was a sure way of getting dumped.

Of course, as soon as Anna ended it, I was desperate to get her back. But Anna wasn't interested, and after a couple of weeks, she was dating someone else.

I'd grown out of lying, but gambling was my forte. I made a mental note to play down my stockbroking.

FOURTEEN

I arrived at the restaurant early, allowing me the pleasure of watching Anna walk in. She looked stunning in her short black dress that led my eyes down to her sexy stockinged legs. She'd tied up her hair, but seductive, red curls dangled down.

'Hi.' I rose and then hung awkward in the air, not brave enough to kiss her hello. I wanted to say how lovely she looked but the words locked in my throat.

'You look smart,' she said.

'Thank you… so do you… I mean, you look great.'

Anna smiled as the waiter pulled out her chair. Once she was settled, we ordered gin and tonic.

'What did you get up to this afternoon?' I said.

'Nothing exciting, just some food shopping. What about you?'

'I worked mainly. I've taken over a major account and need to get up to speed.'

'Sounds impressive.'

The waiter interrupted with menus.

Anna said, 'This place is amazing. I've been wanting to try it for ages. I'm really glad you suggested it.'

'Yeah, it's one of my favourites.' Well, I'd been twice, and both times Philip had paid. Now I noticed the prices, I could see what she meant.

The conversation paused as our drinks arrived and we considered the menu. Anna chose a crab salad followed by chicken, and I went for prawns and a well-done steak. The wine waiter recommended a Burgundy that would complement both the chicken and meat, and I agreed, pretending to know he was right.

Anna raised her glass and gazed over the rim. 'Do you see anyone from university?'

'Not really. I did keep in touch with Colin a bit.' Keeping in touch was stretching it; we'd seen each other about four times. I fidgeted with my napkin, not sure how odd it looked to have no friends from those days.

'Colin Simpson? What's he up to now?'

'He met a thirty-eight-year-old woman with three kids.'

'*What?!*' Her eyes widened. 'How did that go?'

'As far as I know, he's still with her.'

'You are joking! *Colin?*'

'Yup.' I leaned in and let my hand brush against hers as she lowered her glass. She didn't move away.

'He must be mad.'

'Well, we all know that.'

Being with Anna was effortless, and by the second bottle of wine, my eagerness to impress had passed. I told her about my disaster with Keisha and without shame she laughed. Anna also had a string of failed, short relationships and, to my delight, knew the problems of balancing a demanding career with insufficient energy and space. We were just comparing our mutual failures when the conversation turned.

'Do you miss law?' she said.

'Not at all.'

'I don't know much about stockbroking, but it sounds stressful. What's the attraction?'

'Money. Lots of it.'

She slumped back in her chair. 'Really? That's it?'

'I'm looking forward to being a millionaire.'

'Should that impress me?'

My boasting, drunk brain had got it all wrong. 'Well… I don't know.'

'Please tell me there's something else.'

'Okay…' I tried again. 'It's the excitement too. The risk. The thrill of the chase.'

'Have you swallowed a dictionary of clichés with your desert?'

Our laughter pulled it back just as the bill arrived.

'I'll get this,' I said.

'No, I'll pay half.'

'I'm getting it and that's final.'

'Okay, *Mr Millionaire*. Thank you very much, it was lovely.'

'Perhaps you can buy drinks in the pub?' My subtle way of extending the evening.

'Fair enough.' She watched me pick up the bill. 'I'll pop to the ladies' first.'

I counted out enough cash to cover the tip and drank the dregs of the bottle. Anna returned, looking flushed and distracted.

'Peter, I'm really sorry. I'm not feeling well. I think I need to go home.'

'I hope it wasn't the food?'

'No, I don't think so. I'm so, so sorry.'

'Don't apologise, let me take you home.'

'No, it's okay, I just need a taxi. If that's alright?'

'Of course.'

Masking my disappointment, I asked the waiter to call a cab. It arrived within minutes, and with my arm around Anna's waist, I escorted her out.

'I'll call you in the morning to see how you are.'

'Thanks for understanding.'

She was in the cab and out of reach before I could kiss her goodbye. I waved her off, my mood crushed flat, and then caught my own taxi home.

I entered my building and scuffed up the stairs. When my door came into sight, for the first time that evening, I thought of the book. With my breath held, I turned the key in the lock and crept in. The glow of the moon lit the lounge, its honest element bringing comfort and peace, and for the moment, at least, I felt safe.

I poured a nightcap, which turned into two, then three and the fourth one I carried to bed. In my sleep, I stayed watchful, a tiny fraction awake, not entirely convinced I was free.

The next morning, I walked to the phone box to call Anna. She was feeling a bit better but not up for going out. We half-arranged to meet the following Saturday and I promised to call Friday to firm things up. With the day free, I did my usual trick of working solid, and as the afternoon slipped away into evening, I fancied a drop or two, just to oil the cogs.

I grabbed the whisky from the sideboard, but as I unscrewed the bottle, I was conscious of the cupboard and felt the urge to check.

'Bugger it,' I spat, and pulled on the handle but hesitated before I dared to look. My heart beat a little harder.

There was no book.

I needed to get a grip.

I poured the whisky, and a fair measure emptied the bottle. That only lasted a minute, so I scoured the kitchen for something else. I was in luck: a bottle of red wine, left over from Keisha, sat hiding at the back of a cupboard.

The wine kept me company as I poured over figures, and soon, a full bottle was reduced to a glass-stain. I checked the time – it was just past eleven and still early enough to get a good sleep. I packed up my work papers, took my glass to the kitchen and tipsily tottered to bed.

I stirred at five-past-two, needing to pee. I tossed the covers away, hauled myself up and felt drunker than when I'd first come to bed. After stumbling to the toilet, I collapsed back into the sheets and fell dead to the world. But then I woke again, parched, and took a second trip to the bathroom to drink from the tap and have another pee. It was now four-fifteen. Relieved that I could sleep a decent while longer, I sank into a bottomless sleep.

FIFTEEN

I woke with a clear mind, with no sign of the hangover I deserved.

One of the receptionists had beaten me in, and when she looked up to greet me, an odd expression clouded her face. I ignored it and smiled hello.

Around nine, Tom, the finance lead, put his head around the door.

'You'd better get your arse to the partner's premeet.' He nodded towards the boardroom.

'Is there one today?'

'Of course there bloody is.'

'Why wasn't I told? I'm due—'

'Told? What the hell are you talking about?' We stared at each other, neither understanding. 'I'd get a move on, mate.'

Partner premeets were two hours of intense probing and discussion every second Tuesday of the month, requiring painstaking preparation. It was Philip's senior team's chance to impress and arm him with their plans before he met with the other partners. I fumed that the day had been changed without the courtesy of a warning; I needed that time to prepare. I followed Tom out and saw the calendar on Tim's desk – Tuesday 11th January. Tuesday… *Tuesday?*

'It's not bloody Tuesday.' Walking over to Helen's desk, I picked up a *Daily Mail*. It was dated Tuesday 11th January. 'No, no, no!'

'What's wrong?' asked Helen.

'I… Nothing. It's… nothing.'

Bile rose in my throat as I realised what I'd missed from the day before. I'd stood up a key client and now, on top of everything, I was late and unprepared for the partner's premeet.

I grabbed papers that I hoped would help and dashed to the boardroom. I cracked open the door to find Philip in full flow, setting out his expectations. Seeing me, he stopped mid-sentence, his anger charging the atmosphere as all eyes shifted my way. My more sympathetic colleagues squirmed in their seats, while Philip held the silence, waiting for me to sit. I found my seat and tried to disappear into the black leather.

I followed the discussion with the ears and eyes of an endangered predator, determined not to make another mistake. Thinking I'd be prepared, Philip put me on the spot by asking me to go through two accounts in detail. I could just about do them justice. However, my lack of confidence shone as clear as the bewilderment on Philip's face.

The moment we'd finished, I threw myself into recovering my ground. I learned that Ajay and Helen had tried their best to save me, but Philip had wanted projections that only I knew. Philip had blown, sending shrapnel across the team, and they were all still reeling.

When he called me into his office at three-thirty, my heart sank.

'Peter, we need to talk.' He adopted his Everest look – serene, solid and immovable.

'Philip, I'm really sor—'

'You're not yourself lately. I hope you're alright? Anyway, with things as they are, I've had a rethink.'

'Philip—'

'I probably put too much on you.'

'No, Philip… Look, the file last week, that wasn't my fault. And today—'

'What file? Oh, that… I'm not bothered about your bloody filing skills. You missed the Jensen meeting.'

He was a cold-blooded killer, and my panic was rising, 'I know I've messed up, but… I must've caught some kind of virus or something. It's knocked me for six, but I'm over it now.'

'That may be, but I can't afford to take the risk. Sorry, Peter, I've made up my mind. I need to know you can take the pressure. Stepping up isn't easy; there's no disgrace here. You're still young.'

'But—'

'Please, don't embarrass either of us by arguing. I'm not going to change my mind.'

The little boy in me choked down tears of frustration.

'Look, I know you're not yourself. Whatever it is that's bothering you… let's sort it and get you back fighting.'

No, no, no*! You can't shaft me like this, you unsympathetic bastard!* was the scream in my head, but what dribbled out was a pathetic, 'Okay.' I couldn't trust myself to say another word.

'Good man, I knew you'd see it. I'm looking forward to getting the old Peter back.'

Philip looked down at the papers on his desk, giving me the cue to leave. I slunk back to my office, locked the door and collapsed into the chair. There I sat, with my head in my hands, and cried through waves of exhaustion, anger and defeat. When I was all wrung out, I called Sarah.

'Peter, you sound upset.'

I explained about losing my promotion, omitting that I'd somehow missed a whole day – I couldn't get my own head around that yet.

'I thought you were doing really well.'

'I've slipped up a couple of times—'

'A *couple* of times?'

'Yes. It's a big deal here. It's a major step. He needs to be sure.'

'Well, he's a fool and it will serve him right if you go elsewhere.'

If only I wasn't cracking up, I might! 'It's not all bad news. I bumped into Anna Monroe.'

'Anna Monroe?'

'From uni.'

'Is that the Anna who dumped you?' The protective beast had woken.

'Yes, but it wasn't all her.'

'That's not what I remember. You were upset about it for weeks.'

'We've grown up a bit since then.'

'Just be careful. You know how I worry about you. And with everything that's going on with work, please don't overdo it.'

'I won't, I promise.'

I worked until early evening, shutting out the world, soldiering on. Stretching in the chair, I caught my reflection in the window and noticed a feather-light rain dancing in the sky. For a while, I watched patterns forming on the pane, the drizzle transforming into running droplets.

What would my father think now? I thought, and then floated back to a wound. Just for the hell of it, I poked the raw flesh.

We're all there – David, Sarah, Mum and Dad. It's the Rotary Club gala and I'm eight years old. A blazing July day of shorts, dresses, picnics, ice lollies and sticky sun-cream. Rare family time for children of professional workaholics.

Families sat dotted around on tartan rugs in the late-afternoon sunshine, waiting for the competition results. The course, wool rug scratched at my legs, so I sat on the edge, with the dry, summer-scorched grass tickling through my blue sandals.

I'd entered the drawing competition for the under-tens and was desperate to win the prize – a painting set with brushes, watercolours and oils in a smart, wooden case. David was teasing, telling me I'd come last. He'd spent all day in water fights and playing tag with older boys, who refused to let me and my friend, Roland, join in. So, Roland and I entered the competitions and then skimmed stones across the lake. Roland was now with his family, on the other side of the park. Dad wasn't friendly with his dad because he mended cars for a living. That always confused me because it sounded like Roland's dad could do magic, whereas mine worked in a boring office all day.

We sat through what felt like hundreds of prizes – winner of the half-mile dash, through to best Victoria sponge – and then the time came.

'Shush now.' Mum calmed David, who was being even more of a pain than usual in a bid to steal the attention. 'This is it.'

The gala queen, a girl in Sarah's class, stepped forward. She looked down at the paper in her hand, taking what felt like an age to read the name. My heart thumped as I held my breath. Finally, she spoke. 'The winner of the under-ten category is… Peter Tyler!'

'Yeeesssss!' I leapt up, and Mum and Sarah hugged me. David threw his drink on the ground in temper and Dad didn't say a word. But then the authoritative voice of my headmaster, Mr Sharp, the Rotary Club chair, took control of the speakers.

'Apologies, there's been a mistake. Peter *Tyler* came second, so congratulations to Peter for that. The winner is Peter Abbot.' I felt myself colour beetroot and hunched back down on the rug, wanting to disappear.

'Ah-ha-*ha-ha*!' David shouted in my face.

'David, shush. Oh, Peter, you came second, that's brilliant.' Mum wrapped me in her arms.

'Yeah, *se*-cond,' said David, and Sarah thumped his arm.

'I'm so proud—'

'I didn't win!'

Dad stood up. 'Peter, don't be churlish.' *Now* he was interested. 'I think you should go and shake the boy's hand. Let's show there's no hard feelings.'

'Alastair, no.' Mum could see where this was heading.

'Come on. We don't want to make a show of ourselves as bad sports. You've done enough of that already.'

'No! I don't want to.'

'Yes, come on.' He stood, and I squirmed into Mum's arms.

'Alastair—'

'Come on!'

'No! *I don't want to!*' The tears flowed, hot shame on my sunburnt cheeks. The world was laughing at me.

Dad stood sneering, not hiding his disgust. 'Peter, you're such an embarrassment.'

Peter, you're such an embarrassment… The words echoed in my twenty-five-year-old brain. And today he'd be embarrassed again.

With my taste for work spoilt, I packed up and left. Rain had dampened the streets to grey and cars scuttled in little bursts between the traffic-light changes, like tin beetles trying to find the shelter of home. By the time I re-emerged from the tube, the rain had stopped but the wet air enhanced the chill. I pulled my coat lapels up to my face and marched to the off-licence to buy whisky. With the bottle tucked safely under my arm, I pressed on towards home.

I closed the outside door on the cold and climbed the stairs with a stamp, to get some warmth to my feet. I turned through the last run of staircase and stopped dead. The door to my flat stood half-open.

'What the hell...'

I inched forwards, my eyes fixed on the black of the lobby and blood thumping in my ears. I raised my hand and pushed the door wider.

'Hello?'

Holding the whisky bottle by the neck, I sidled towards the doorway. The door slammed in my face, missing me by fractions and fanning my hair. I grabbed and pushed down on the handle, but the door didn't budge. Stepping back, I delved in my pocket for keys and bungled them onto the floor.

'Shit!' I swooped down, and at the same time, the door clicked and opened in one, smooth arc.

Still on my haunches, I looked up.

Then I heard it – a low scraping from the far side of the flat, the drag of a weight along the floor. Gradually, it drew closer and closer.

I tried to stand, but my jelly legs froze. Terror rose to my throat and my thin, strangled cry died in the air. And then the noise stopped. And I stared into absolute nothing, as I squatted, shaking, rooted to the spot.

A crackle of lightning lit a pair of eyes, sending me howling to the floor.

I scrambled to my feet and snatched on the light. Whatever had been there was gone. I burst into the lounge and checked every corner. I paced to the kitchen, then the bedroom and the bathroom. I found nothing. Shaking, I poured a whisky, drank it down in two gulps and then poured more. With the third in my hand, I sank to the floor.

Of course that mumbo-jumbo didn't work – what the hell was I thinking? I went to down that third drink and stopped. My eyes fixed on something under the table. It had fallen from the pages and had fluttered out of sight. I scrambled to get it and stared at the words:

'Mr & Mrs E H Featherstone, 15 Dawson Road Kensington.'
'Find me in death – bye, bye.'

'Fifteen Dawson Road,' I repeated in my head.

Fired up for the challenge, I shot to my feet and went to fetch my street map. I checked the index and then flicked to the page. My anxious eyes took a moment to find it, but there it was, not far from Kensington tube. I had to try something to solve this and would go there straight after work.

SIXTEEN

It was another new day in the land of opportunity, and I woke in discomfort, curled awkwardly on the sofa. I'd drank too much and had fallen asleep. My shirt felt sticky from night sweats; my greasy hair was as dark as the shadow on my face. From the ceiling rose, artificial light burned, creating a mirror of the sad scene in the un-curtained windows.

I forfeited a much-needed bath, made coffee, then took off my jacket and shirt and shaved in my vest. I rubbed my hair through in a sink of warm water, scrubbed it with a towel and combed it into place. After re-dressing, I picked up the business card and left.

At work I went through the motions, trying to focus my sluggish, distracted brain. Time dragged until the markets closed, until I was free to leave for Dawson Road. Pulling on my coat, I almost reached the door.

'Peter, come and join us,' Philip called, and my heart sank to my boots when I saw Ajay and Alan, the senior analyst, walking into Philip's office. Alan always took an hour to warm up, before making the same point in ten different ways with pictures, charts, tables, and graphs. It was the death knell to my plans and my whole body sighed as I took off my coat and joined them.

The minutes drained away as we ran through several sets of far-fetched scenarios, just for the sheer fun. I watched the world darkening, itching to get out. In futile attempts to close down conversations, I made offers to research things later, to meet with Alan separately and re-do reports the next day. Still the meeting crept on. I saw two hours tick away, realising that a third would see my plans abandoned, leaving me to face another night of hell.

Ajay nudged me to say, '*Concentrate, boss!*', his loyalty strained to its limits. I saw him assessing the cost of sticking with me, wondering if it was time to move on. I sensed that change across the team too. I was letting them down and becoming a risk; I was no longer the legend they believed in. But I couldn't fight everything and needed to stretch their patience a few degrees more.

At the close of the meeting, I made straight for the door.

'It was a good meeting. I think we're nearly there.' I turned and saw Philip angling for a chat. Ajay had stayed in his chair.

'Yes, I'll do these things first thing tomorrow.'

'We could go through some of it now.'

'No, really, I've got it. I made copious notes.' He raised a brow. 'I need to catch a train.'

'Oh.'

Ajay said, 'Shall we go over it and I'll catch up with Peter in the morning?'

'No, there's not much point in that.'

I sensed Ajay's rejection and couldn't help feeling pleased. I nodded and left them to chat.

I started towards the tube and then had second thoughts and flagged a cab. This wasn't a night to scrimp on a taxi fare.

The meter ticked the pounds away, but instead of fretting, I focused on my task. I imagined myself meeting the residents of Dawson Road and wondered what I could say to them: 'Hello, is this your business card? I found it in a haunted book.' I had to do better than that. Something, somehow had to click into place and I'd just have to go with my gut.

We circled Hyde Park and then entered the residences around Kensington. The streets grew grander, greener, cleaner, showing off broad bay-windowed houses that hogged the premium space.

At the start of Dawson Road, I climbed out of the cab. There were thirtyish terraced villas framed behind waist-high front garden walls. Each house had two upper floors and sizeable basements that peeped out into the street. Their numbers followed in order, house after house, not evens on one side and odds on the other. Number fifteen was the last but one on the left-hand side, before a road junction.

Despite the hour, the front curtains were open, and the house was in complete darkness. For the first time it dawned on me that the owners might be out. I pushed open the metal gate, walked up a weed-invaded path and climbed six stone steps to the door. I rapped the brass knocker three times and, after no answer, rapped it again.

My heart sank at the prospect of waiting, and, hopeful for any sign of life, I stretched to see into the front bay window. From what I could tell, the room looked empty. I stooped to peer into the basement but felt someone watching me. I looked up and saw a face in the bedroom window and jumped at the shock. Then I realised it was only a trick of the light and there was nobody there.

The house was not giving up its secrets without persuasion. I don't know how I thought of it, through intuition or desperation, but I decided to try round the back. I walked to the footpath and followed it past number sixteen, to the street at the end of Dawson Road. A few yards later, I'd found the alleyway that ran behind the houses.

The streetlights made no impact on the black tunnel of passage. As I looked to pick my way, a couple crossed the road towards me. I deflected my interest by looking at my watch, making out that I was struggling to see the hands in the darkness. However, they walked straight past without taking any notice, wrapped up in their chat.

I edged my way alongside a six-foot wall and passed a wooden gate. I walked to the next gate, which I knew would be number fifteen. I snicked the catch and pushed.

Steep, flagged steps led down to a basement-level back door. I followed the slippery trail, grasping onto a slimy, wooden handrail and carefully placing my feet. When I safely reached the last step, I let my eyes adjust to the path before moving to the door. A top panel of frosted glass prevented me from looking in, but as I peered closer, I could see that the lock had already been forced. I pushed, and the door swung open.

'Hello,' I called, and waited. There was no response.

I stood locked in a dilemma. I had no legitimate reason to go inside; I'd be trespassing for the craziest of reasons. I gazed once more at the freedom of the garden and then stepped in through the door.

I left the door an inch short of its frame, just in case. I could make out a cavernous, outdated kitchen with a butler sink and a mishmash of stand-alone cupboards and dressers. I found the light and switched it on to show a staircase to my left and then what looked like an under-stair cupboard door. Beyond that, towards the front on the house and facing me was another door. I crept towards it and listened, and once I was sure, I pulled it open. Damp, fusty air escaped as I saw through the shadows to make out living quarters that had been unused for years. A sad chair sat by an empty fireplace and a bed lay naked in the corner.

I closed the door and turned to the stairs. I stood at the first step for a second, deciding whether to go up, the uneasiness tickling my skin.

'Hello,' I called. After hearing nothing, I climbed.

The stairs curled up into a corridor and I found myself standing opposite the main entrance to the house. Shining through the front door's fanlight, the streetlamp filled the space well enough for me to see. I was standing in a hallway of doors.

'Anyone here?' My voice echoed into silence. I put my hand on the light switch but then changed my mind about signalling my presence, and so I tiptoed in shadow down towards the front door. On my left, the main staircase ascended, and I followed it up with my eyes. The stairs disappeared into a blackness that I didn't dare stare at for long.

Moving back, I opened the door into the front room and found it almost bare. An armchair stood proud in the middle of the floor and several boxes lined the walls. Someone was moving out.

I went along to the next door, which revealed a dining table and chairs. Then I opened the last door, at the back of the house, where it felt safe to turn on the light. The room smelled of old tobacco but felt soulless and cold. I found more stacked boxes and a desk by the window. I flipped back the lid of the nearest box and uncovered newspaper-wrapped ornaments. In the next, I found framed photographs and slid one out. A man and woman stood arm in arm on a pier: the man's handsome face beamed with laughter, while the woman's hat hid everything except her smile. I considered them for a moment – had I found the owners? Intruding on them no longer, I returned them to their den.

I crossed the threadbare, patterned carpet to the desk. On top sat a cardboard box full of official-looking paperwork. The top document was a bank statement belonging to a Mrs Faye Featherstone. My heart thumped with adrenalin.

'Featherstone,' I breathed. 'I've found you.'

Excited, I searched for more clues amongst the statements and bills, and at the bottom of the pile, I found a business card. I picked it up and read: '*Marshall Winter, Probate Specialists*'.

'Oh, that doesn't sound good.'

I tossed the card back into the box and moved on to the desk's top drawer, which was chock full of matches, jars of ink, scissors and pens. The second drawer was empty apart from three forgotten paper clips. When I tugged at the deeper, third drawer, it rolled out smoothly on its runners, revealing a stash of documents, letters and envelopes. I lifted the top papers to see the layers underneath and then caught sight of a bundle of letters. I pulled them free.

'Oh, lord, I've struck gold.' They were all addressed to Mr E Featherstone.

As I slid back the drawer, it jammed. I reversed the drawer out and reached in behind it, squeezing my arm through as far as I could. The tips of my fingers brushed against something, paper teasing me, just out of reach. I pushed to stretch a touch further and the drawer scraped pain through my wrist. With one last thrust, I grabbed hold and brought out a black, leather-bound book.

Just then, a creak, like a foot on a floorboard, sounded directly above. I listened for another but heard nothing more.

Must be the sounds of the house, I thought, and turned my attention back to my treasure. My drawer jamming had spoilt the leather cover with a deep, ugly crease. I opened it and turned the dry pages to slanted, spidery handwriting that said: '*Edward Featherstone, 1st January 1938*'.

My visit was far from hopeless.

I moved to sit on the desk, but a heavier creak stopped me dead. I waited, barely breathing.

And then I heard it, from somewhere upstairs, a scraping sound. A noise that scratched through my body, tormenting my screaming nerves.

I scrambled to get out, grabbing the letters and notebook. I rushed into the hallway and smacked straight into a weight that knocked me flying onto the floor. Dazed, I made sense of barging into another human being. Footsteps ran on ahead and then downstairs to the basement and out the back door.

I staggered to my feet, my hand throbbing from its whack on the floor. I made for the stairs, down to the kitchen and, at mid-way to the outside door, froze. Something was behind me.

It willed me to turn, but my terrified heart wouldn't let me. I had to get out or be trapped. Then a sweet, sickening odour caught in my throat and the air felt too thin to breathe. My head spun and, on the verge of collapse, I made one last push for the door.

SEVENTEEN

I can't remember ever feeling as cold as I did that evening.
The gloom of that house invaded my body with a chill I
couldn't fight. At Angel, the rain bounced and drenched,
but instead of craving home, I dreaded its cold, empty
welcomings. Up ahead, The Earl's warm glow beckoned.

A straggle of locals propped up the bar, inspecting my
pint and medicinal whisky. Thankfully, the fire was lit, so
I took the table near it, hauled off my heavy, wet overcoat
and draped it over a chair to dry off. For five minutes I
sat, staring into the flames, while the whisky fought back
in shivery bursts. I relived my last moments in the house
and shuddered. Whoever that was – a snooper, a squatter,
a burglar – they must have been there the whole time. And
the scare they'd given me had shot me to pieces – the house
had really got to my nerves.

And now I'd stolen, and intentionally stolen, someone
else's stuff.

I tugged the notebook from my pocket, looked at its
gloomy, black cover and sighed. As innocent as it seemed,
I just knew it was trouble. I stretched the book open and
flicked past Edward's name. The same spidery handwriting

filled page upon page, words teetering forwards in their haste to be said. It looked an unappetising test for sore eyes, but I turned to the start and began.

The first entries flowed like a diary.

> *1st January. Fate has forced my hand. I had hoped to share my legacy with confidence and wit, boasting out my accomplishments. Time, however, has cheated me of that.*
>
> *George has drawn up a trust fund for Ned, which I will leave in his care. At last I have done something good.*
>
> *4th January. I walked out into the grey, miserable morning and headed to Hyde Park. I stood on the banks of the Serpentine and stared into the icy water. An hour slipped by. An hour of feeling completely numb.*

The cryptic sentences piqued my interest; I turned the page and read on.

> *7th January. Faye, I am a tortured man. I cannot go on. I have tried so hard to wait for Ned. But the pain is too much to bear. You are my only hope.*
>
> *If my miserable existence is to have any point at all, I need Ned to know. I need him to understand. Please make sure that he gets this book.*
>
> *You have no reason to offer me mercy, yet still I press on you with my selfish demands. As your husband, you are bound to me by earthly law. Do this final thing for me. Do all that you can for Ned to read these words.*
>
> *If you deny me this kindness, I pray that your soul will not rest.*

The unrest in my own soul struck such a chord that the hairs stood on the back of my neck. I turned the page, eager to meet what came next and saw that the writing changed into a memoir. The close sentences were even harder to track but I focused my eyes and read on.

I, Edward Henry Featherstone, was born in Kensington on 3rd February 1888, the only child of Edward Robert and Gertrude Esther Featherstone (formerly Ingham). My father was a talented architect who designed houses for wealthy businessmen and high-society clients. He was a shrewd man who dined on the privileges of money and invested wisely to ensure its continuous supply. My father had high hopes for his son; however, his overindulgences only encouraged me to be lazy and wasteful. Spoilt, headstrong, handsome, young men do not make the best achievers.

I endured school at Harrow and went on to study history at St John's College, Oxford. I was bright but not a natural student, preferring social gaieties to dry studies and college dust.

I skimmed on a couple of pages.

I met Faye at the university boat race. She was the sister of my friend, the rower Albert Robinson, and had come with their parents to cheer him along. When she smiled, a lightning bolt struck my heart. She was playful and aware of her charms, and rather than shy away, she seemed as drawn to me as I to her. We flirted all afternoon and when the time was right, I asked her to join me for a walk the following Sunday. From there our intimate acquaintance grew as we enjoyed the unusually hot summer, the soaring temperatures in tune with our thirst for love.

We wanted to marry, before our passions courted scandal. My proposal caused a stink with Faye's father, a businessman who had clawed his way to the top. He wanted Faye to marry upwards, instead of gambling on a fellow fresh out of university, with only looks and charm to his name. It was a stark but fair assessment. He made it clear that under no circumstances would he give us his blessing to marry.

Despite it all, we married on 13th April 1912, two days before the Titanic sank (if there should be a better omen). We honeymooned in the lakes and then moved into Dawson Road. The place was too much for my bank clerk's salary, but my father bought the place outright. Faye had chosen the house for the garden and spent countless happy hours fashioning it into her sanctuary, where she created the most magnificent displays of flowers and plants.

Year after year passed with Faye and I devoted, yet without her bearing a child. I faced being the end of the Featherstone line. My disappointment pushed us apart and we diverted our energies and frustrations elsewhere. Faye poured her efforts into charity work, helping children who would become her surrogate family, and I became a local MP.

My infidelity was only a matter of time, driven by our changing desires. We were due to attend a charity ball when a headache kept Faye at home. Refusing to give up on the evening, I went alone, knowing there would be friends there to keep me company. When I danced with Katherine Bell, the daughter of financier Charles Bell, I was captivated. Through the evening we found a connection, a teasingly dangerous attraction.

With Katherine, my life found new meaning. I truly loved Faye, but Katherine had fire and desired me in a way that Faye never could. Every second in Katherine's presence was a thrill, and every day brought joy and excitement. Katherine was an honest soul, and of course, after three months of our secrecy, she demanded that I should come clean.

Without doubt, I was intensely in love with Katherine, yet I still cared deeply for Faye. I knew that Faye would be heartbroken and humiliated if I left her, and everything we had built would be gone. I was torn in two and tormented by thoughts of losing one or the other. In the end, I saw sense and realised that I was living in a dream. One day, the lovely, spirited Katherine, would tire of an old bore like me.

I arranged to meet Katherine at our usual hotel, to tell her my decision. I was about to carry out the bitter deed, when Katherine burst into tears and told me that she was pregnant. In an instant, my world turned upside down. To abandon Katherine when she was having my child felt impossible. Fate had dealt the one card that had sealed Faye's undoing.

This was more like the thriller I wanted. I paused to get myself another pint, then settled down to read.

I planned things out meticulously, obsessed with being fair, as if the salvation of my soul depended upon it. I drew up a monthly allowance for Faye, ensuring she had everything she needed. I thought that distance would be wise, and through an old university friend, I found accommodation and employment in Edinburgh.

For the time being, I withdrew from public attention and resigned my post as a local MP.

On a perfect late-summer evening, the air rich with honeysuckle and jasmine, I walked home to Dawson Road. To this day, the memory of opening the door and seeing Faye burns vivid. Her face was scarlet with rage, and she launched her attack before I could make sense of it. The day's post had brought a letter from George Locke, my solicitor, and knowing in her bones that something was afoot, Faye had opened it. Detailed inside was the settlement I had put in place for her. Fuelled by her find, Faye had ripped apart my study to find all other letters on the matter. She had uncovered my affair and plans with Katherine.

There was no point in lying to Faye and, in truth, I welcomed the relief of getting the whole thing out into the open. I confessed that Katherine and I were leaving for Edinburgh, where I had found a new job and home. Surprisingly, Faye took it well, knowing deep down that we were finished. But then I mentioned the baby.

It took a few moments for my confused mind to catch up. Faye had not realised that Katherine was pregnant. She went crazy, howling like a wounded animal, the pain of the past ten years exploding from her heart. She threatened that if I did not leave Katherine, she would make the affair public, and everyone would know that Charles Bell had brought up a whore who was now expecting his illegitimate grandchild. Faye knew, with Charles Bell's reputation tainted, he would have me ruined and out of his daughter's life.

I refused to bow down to Faye's blackmail and be punished for her barren body. Furious, I stormed out of the house.

The bell clanged for last orders, and I weighed up buying another pint or going out into the cold. I decided to brave the inevitable, for the lure of a nightcap at home. I wrapped my coat around me, the inside radiating warmth from the fire, giving me heart to hit the road.

Walking along the quiet streets, I listened to the echo of my feet. But then there was another step, from someone behind. I turned to look but saw no one. I rushed on and the footsteps still followed. I spun to catch my stalker out. But the street was empty. Confused and lacking in bravery, I quickened my pace to get home.

By habit, I clicked on the gas fire and glugged whisky into a glass. I took the bottle and placed it on the coffee table with the book, then hung up my scarf and coat. I settled in my armchair and drank down the full glass. Past caring about the consequences, I poured an inch more and started reading from where I'd left off.

Katherine was staying with her cousin, Hilda, in Belgravia. From there, she could prepare to leave without raising her parents' suspicions. As my cab neared Hilda's, the enormity of my actions weighed heavy, and an unexpected remorse took hold. I panicked, my shirt collar choking me, as I realised how much I was giving up. The cab rolled in front of Hilda's door and the driver waited for his money. In that moment, I decided to end it. Yet I could not slink away like a coward; I had to let Katherine know. I considered the house with a new sense of dread and paid the driver his fare.

On seeing me in such a sorry state, Katherine could not hide her shock. Over a welcome stiff whisky, I unravelled the story of how Faye had discovered our plans. Katherine treated me so lovingly that all my doubts about us melted away. She suggested that we should depart for Edinburgh the very next day. I said it was too soon, but when that troubled Katherine, I gave in and agreed. It meant going back to Dawson Road and collecting some essentials. Wanting to get that over with, I kissed Katherine a sweet kiss goodbye and promised to return soon.

Faye of course pleaded with me to stay. She asked me to remember our happier times and promised we would have them again. I nearly broke, but from the depths of my boots, I found a cold, cruel strength and stepped out of the house for good.

I soared like an eagle, broken free from my fetters and flying on the wings of relief. My high spirits were flattened, however, when no one answered Hilda's door. I pounded at the unyielding wood, panic rising as I tried to make sense of it. I figured I had misunderstood, and that Katherine had retired early, to be ready to leave the next day.

To avoid going back to Dawson Road, I went to George's. He kindly plied me with brandy, and from the comfort of George's study, the mix-up with Katherine seemed obvious enough.

I returned to Hilda's early the next morning. This time a young maid answered and said that Hilda and Katherine had left for the country. Losing control, I demanded to know where they had gone, bullying the girl to go inside and enquire. After several long minutes, she informed me that Hilda and Katherine were at Mistlegrove, the Hampshire family home.

Confused, I needed to get to Mistlegrove swiftly. Before then, though, I had to face the reality of returning home. I expected Faye to behave all self-righteously and braced myself for the humiliation. To my surprise, Faye was pleased to see me and acted pitifully on her best behaviour, as if by being good she could repair our love. Emotionally drained by it all, I refused to be drawn into any conversation and moved my things into the guest room.

I travelled to Mistlegrove the next day. The butler showed me in, and as we passed through the magnificent hall, my heart leapt with the thought of seeing Katherine. At the other side of the drawing room door, however, it was her father, the grim Charles Bell, who waited instead.

Charles's mere presence dominated the room, sending a tremble through my nerves. As his tight eyes scrutinised me, I felt like a man about to duel. Through the sneer on his lips, he demanded to know what business I had calling unannounced on his daughter. I stumbled to apologise for my 'spur-of-the-moment' visit, and he spat that I had wasted my time because Katherine was in London with her cousin.

It was then that I realised they were all in it together. I was a fool to think that Hilda was on our side, when all along, it had been a plan to get Katherine away from me. And no doubt Charles was the mastermind, protecting his daughter and his own reputation. I left him to his miserable afternoon and returned to London, more determined than ever to find and rescue Katherine.

When I tried Hilda's again, I was shown in to see the wretched woman herself. She claimed not to know Katherine's whereabouts. She expected me to believe that it was Katherine who would not answer the door that night and had invented the lie about Mistlegrove. Hilda had travelled with her to stay with their aunt in Tunbridge before Katherine had travelled on alone.

I marched home, seething and unwavering about beating the Bell family at its own spiteful game. When I arrived at the house, a letter waited for me. I tore it open.

The very letter was tucked inside the notebook:

My Dearest Edward,

I am sorry for leaving you so suddenly and hope you will find it in your heart to forgive me. Seeing you tormented and torn in two was so very painful.

It sounds so wonderful and easy to move away and start over again; however, you would lose everything you have worked so hard for. My father has many powerful friends and would use all his influence to destroy you. We could never have the life of which we dreamed. We have been fooling ourselves and now it is time to wake up, before everything is lost.

The scandal of an illegitimate child will destroy my family. For them, there will be only one solution – to have our baby in secret and then give it up. I could never do that. Therefore, I will go away to have our baby and start a new life on my own, somewhere I am not known.

Please do not worry about me, I am safe and will take good care of our child. Try to continue with your life as it was before. I know you will achieve great things. It is because of this, and my deep love for you, that I can bear this heart-breaking deed.

I will write to you once more when our baby is born, to let you know all is well.

All my love,
Katherine

The words felt detached and cold, not the voice of the Katherine I knew. I cursed myself for turning up in such a state that night, with my wavering intentions. Those crucial moments had sealed my ruin.

With Katherine gone, I was forced to rebuild my life. I reclaimed my post at the bank and welcomed the mundane structure that allowed me to sleepwalk through a hollow existence. Faye and I suffered, side by side, in a loveless pretence. I felt the hope within Faye, but I was a broken man with no interest in our marriage. I struggled through the days, just living for Katherine's next letter. It arrived five months later:

Dear Edward,

I hope that this letter finds you safe and well.

Three weeks ago, on the 28th of July, I gave birth to our baby boy. I have named him Edward Arthur, after you, of course. I call him Ned, as that seems to suit him well. He is perfect and healthy and has your eyes.

Please know for sure that I will always love you and no one will ever replace you in my heart. Many times, I have agonised about coming back, but it would be selfish and unfair of me to upset your life now, and I must learn to accept that.

Be happy to know that everything is going well for me and I am settled in my new life with our beautiful boy.

I will not disturb you again, so goodbye, Edward. I send you all my love and wish you the very best in life.

Ever yours,
Katherine

I had a son! Edward Arthur. Ned. My heart swelled to burst at the thought of him. I felt desperate to meet him, to hold him, to protect him.

And more than that, Katherine still wanted me.

I checked back at the letter and, of course, there was no address. I looked at the postmark and my heart fell through the floor. It read, 'New York, USA'. It was a piercing blow. I sat with my head in my hands, letting the enormity of the distance sink in. But, in a rush of fire, I refused to let go. Regardless of effort or expense, I swore to find Katherine and Ned.

I called into the club and shared my news with George, hoping he might offer some advice. Better than that, he offered his services to search on my behalf. Never did a fellow have a better friend. George and I chatted long into the night, and in the morning, he set to work.

George felt sure we would have swift success. That optimism, however, proved false, as one by one, his investigations failed. The months ticked by without success and then turned into years. I can honestly say we tried everything, but Katherine got her way.

I have punished Faye for her part in my downfall and have been guilty of many affairs. In my lowest moment, I seduced the housekeeper, Dorothy, sharing a bed right under Faye's nose. And now when I think of Katherine, it is with the shame of the man I have become.

Every day is a torment and I refuse to carry on.

Ned's understanding and forgiveness is my soul's only hope.

And that was the end of the account.

My drunken mind tried to make sense of my thoughts. Edward had demanded Faye's help, but it was me that was being plagued. Was finding Ned now my problem? Had Edward lured me into this nightmare, through a random book, so I'd carry on with the search?

Surely, that was ridiculous.

It became too much to think about, and in five hours, I was due back at work. Knowing I'd be facing the meanest of hangovers, I gave in and went to bed.

EIGHTEEN

Reading Edward's notebook left me in a strange, dark mood that I struggled to shake. I resented his sly invasion into my life. I resented being controlled. Since finding the book, I'd lost Keisha, my promotion, my credibility with Philip and my team. I just wanted my old life back, to be 'Peter Tyler, Master Stockbroker of the Universe' without any distractions. But I was being forced to do what Edward Featherstone wanted, whoever he was. I was being forced to find a stranger in America who no one else could find. And if I didn't find him soon, what would I lose next?

And time spent on Edward's search was more time diverted from work. Which was it going to be? Goose chase and the sack, or a ghost wreaking havoc... and then the sack? Yes, I was screwed.

For the rest of the week, at least, I managed to push it all to the back of my mind and immerse myself in work, promising Edward, with my fingers crossed behind my back, that the weekend was better for leisurely spiritualism.

When Friday evening arrived, I planned to stay late again, but Ajay looked in.

'Boss, I know what you're planning, but you need to slow down.'

'I need to get this done.'

'Yeah, and a rest from it will help.' He closed the door and came over, lowering his voice. 'The team are moaning about you. You hardly give them the time of day.'

'I think we all know I've been up against it lately.'

'Yeah, we do. But all this is bad for morale.'

'What, me not going to the pub and getting pissed with them?'

'All I'm saying is… this is a time when you need your team behind you. We want to be there for you, but you won't let us in. When you're on top, we're on top.'

He was right and I hated him for it.

'Come on, pack up. We're going out.'

So, instead of another night of graft, I joined Ajay, Helen, Dan and Tim, and let my coiled spring explode. Dan set the genius challenge of hitting one pub every twenty minutes, and two hours in, it wasn't pretty. It was too much, too fast and when the fresh air hit me after leaving bar seven, I threw up over Tim's shoes. My night of bonding ended with Helen bundling me into a taxi home.

I woke with an outrageous hangover and lay in bed dying. Just as I was slipping back into unconsciousness, a panic pierced the pounding – I'd forgotten about Anna.

I forced myself out of bed and clung on as my head throbbed with every movement and a wave of nausea rolled through my throat. I dragged on jeans and a jumper and then trundled to the kitchen, where I clicked on the kettle and spattered coffee granules into a mug, straight from the jar. When the boiling water hit the coffee, I retched with the smell and staggered out to the sofa.

I sprawled out in death, half dozing, for a good thirty minutes. Eventually the thought of Anna pierced through, and I pulled myself round so I could call her. Hurting, I dragged on a coat, checked my pocket for change and risked the expedition.

The Saturday morning streets semi-slumbered and pushy, week-day commuters had transformed into joggers and people sauntering to the shop. When I reached the phone box, the effort of heaving the rigid, weighted door brought a twang of pain from my arm muscles up into my brain.

I dialled, and after five rings, Anna answered. I pushed in my ten-pence piece.

'Hi, it's Peter.'

'Oh, you've not forgotten me then?'

'Sorry… it was manic all day…'

'It's fine, I'm only teasing.'

'You sound better. Are you okay to meet up?'

'Yes. I don't know what it was. I've been fine all week.'

Lucky you. The smell of the phone box – urine, damp and cigarettes – was turning my stomach again. 'How about a walk later?'

'And lunch? My turn to pay.'

'Okay.'

'I could meet you outside Green Park tube at twelve?'

'Can you make it one? I just need to finish something.' *Recovering.*

'Yes, see you then.'

Two lots of painkillers failed to shift my suffering and I waited at Green Park wishing I'd put Anna off. Five minutes after me, she spewed out of the tunnel with a burst of travellers.

'Hi,' I said, and, starting like I meant to go on, planted a firm kiss on her cool cheek.

'Isn't it lovely?' she said. The sun pierced through the cloud but not through the chill.

'I wish I'd worn a warmer coat.' Alcohol sweats had fooled me, and the cold was worsening my mood.

'Oh, do you want to find a café?'

'No, I'll warm up. Let's walk towards St James's.' Before I strode off, she caught my arm and linked it.

'Have you had a good week? How's that new account?'

'Err… it's… yeah, it's good.' My head banged.

'You don't sound too sure about it!' She laughed.

'What've you been up to?' I changed the subject.

'My sister visited, and we went shopping for baby clothes. She's due in—'

'It was just a short bug then?' My timing was off, and Anna's face showed it.

'Yes, I told you. It was just a twenty-four-hour thing.'

'Oh, yes, sorry.' Anna stayed quiet. I looked up to the sky. 'Feels like the weather's turning. I bet it's frosty later.'

'If you're cold, I don't mind—'

'I'll be alright.'

Anna smiled and pulled her link around me tighter, trying to keep me warm. 'A friend of mine has an interview at yours.'

'Montgomery's?'

'Oh no, I meant Tyler's. He's a solicitor.'

'Oxbridge, I hope?'

'No, a dumbo from Bristol.' Like *her*, she meant.

'Sorry, I didn't mean—'

'It's okay. No offence taken.'

'I don't know what's wrong with me.'

'Come on, I'll cheer you up.'

I didn't let on it was a hangover and endeavoured snap out of my mood. I picked my words more carefully as we chatted and walked around the lake in St James's Park, through Horse Guard's Parade and onto the Embankment. When we reached Northumberland Avenue, Anna suggested lunch and we found a traditional-looking Italian towards the Strand.

The café was packed, and the soundtrack of chatter played havoc with my head. We both ordered the pasta special – tagliatelle with mushrooms and pancetta – and a bottle of Classico Soave. I couldn't believe the alcohol tempted me when I felt so bad, but it did. The wine came and Anna tasted it, nodding to the waiter to say it was okay. As soon as my glass was poured, I took a deep swig, wincing behind my hand at its sourness.

'Do you own the flat you live in?' I asked.

'Yes.'

'In Camden? You must be doing alright.'

'My father paid the deposit.'

'Ah. Well, in a few months I plan to buy something outright in Islington.' I sat back and steepled my hands. 'I like Islington – it's got a good feel to it. It'll do nicely for now. I should've done it before, really, but I've been too busy to look.'

'Uh-hmm.'

'I might buy somewhere else too, as an investment.'

'Sounds like a good idea.' She didn't seem impressed.

'Yeah, well, it makes sense to build up as much as you can. And I can. Anyway, you must get paid a fair bit?'

'I'm not that interested in the money side.'

'It's a major part of it, though, isn't it? I mean, no one works for free.'

She looked away, and I'd lost her, but then she said, 'Do you do anything other than work?'

'Oh…' Knocked off kilter, I stared at my glass for inspiration and rode a wave of hangover head-pounding.

'It can't be all that excites you.' She wiggled towards me in her seat, encouraging.

The only thing coming to mind was Edward, but with great timing the pasta arrived. I bought some time as the waiter laid down two heaped plates. He brought over the parmesan and black pepper, and after refilling our glasses, left.

Anna still stared expectantly. 'Well?'

I wiped my mouth with the red paper napkin and looked up to gauge her. 'You might not believe it.'

'Try me.'

'Okay. A few weeks ago, I got involved in…' I paused.

'Hmm?'

'A *personal* case.' Very inventive. 'I'm trying to trace the relatives of a client and… well, let's say it's been a bit of treasure hunt.'

'I didn't know you did that sort of thing.'

'Usually I don't.'

'You're being very cagey. Is it another woman?'

'No! It's just someone who can't make contact himself.'

'Why's that?'

'Because… he's dead.' I hoped to interest Anna with that nugget but instead she looked angry, thinking I was mocking her.

'Good luck with *that*!' She lifted her bag onto her knee and rummaged inside for distraction. She brought out a tissue and rubbed her nose.

'Anna, I know it sounds mad. That's why I wouldn't say. But honestly, there's been all sorts of weird stuff happening. I'm not messing around. It would be good to share it with someone.'

She considered me for several seconds. 'Okay, tell me more. But it better not be a joke.'

'I promise, it's not.'

I filled her in on everything that had happened. I let it all out and she didn't interrupt. When I'd finished, she stared at me, frowning, the face she pulled when deep in thought. 'So, who was hiding in the house?'

'I have no idea.'

'You could have been killed.'

'I nearly was. I've got a very bruised backside.'

'And you've not read the letters yet?'

'No. I'd just… I'd had enough. I'm knackered with it all, to be honest, and need to focus on work.'

'I can't believe you! I'd be so curious.' She drained her glass. 'Come on, let's go and read them.' She went into her bag again and took twenty pounds from her purse.

'Let me get this,' I said.

'No, back off!' She slapped the note down.

I smiled and did what I was told.

NINETEEN

When Anna stepped into my flat, she wasn't impressed. I'd raised her expectations of where rich city boys lived, and clearly, this wasn't it. She perched on the edge of the sofa, as if sitting on it would dirty her dress. I hurried to gather a collection of dirty mugs and plates, and ferried them into the kitchen.

I laid out Edward's notebook and letters, and left Anna to study them while I made coffee.

'We'll need a pad and pen,' she called. 'We'll make notes as we go along.'

Bringing everything over, I settled down next to her. 'There you go, madam.'

Each letter was addressed to 'Mr E Featherstone' in the same handwriting. They had all been deftly sliced open and, apart from a bit of browning, looked in mint condition.

'From this first letter,' Anna flattened it out, 'we know that the sender was indeed Katherine.' I wasn't amazed so far. 'They all have a Boston, USA, postmark. The earliest is dated 1927, and the latest… 1933.'

'And there are two letters for every year, July and December,' I added.

'Write all that down, Sherlock.'

'Ah, you know… I think Ned was born in July.' I checked Edward's notebook. 'Yes. Katherine wrote at Christmas and Ned's birthday.'

'Very good. So, the first is stamped 11th December 1927. Let's start reading.' Anna rubbed her hands together in hammed-up glee.

We took it in turns to read each letter out loud. In the first, Katherine said she'd wrestled with whether to write but felt she should share news about Ned. She and Ned were living with a friend in Boston, and she hoped to find their own apartment soon.

By the second letter, Katherine and Ned had moved, and she was working in a department store. Ned was nearing his first birthday and had taken his first steps. By the third letter, Katherine felt settled in Boston and was looking forward to Christmas. The next two letters followed in the same way, sharing snippets of banal news.

'This is better.' Anna was on the sixth letter. Katherine confessed that she couldn't bear it any longer and wanted Edward to write. She shared her address and explained that she'd changed her name to Katherine Clayton, to prevent being tracked.

We stared at each other, both thinking the same. I took the letter from Katherine to read the words myself. 'All that energy and expense wasted on searching, when here, in black and white, is Katherine's address and new name.'

'Now we know for sure that Edward never saw these letters. There's a story there!' Anna took back the letter and laid it on the table.

'That'll be Faye, of course. That's some feat, keeping these hidden. Edward must've walked around with his eyes closed.'

'I suppose when you're not expecting to see something, it's easy to miss.'

In the next letter, Katherine appealed for Edward's mercy, begging him to get in touch. A letter later, December 1931, she vowed to keep writing, in the hope that one day he would change his mind and reply. However, July 1933 was the final letter. Katherine had given no hint that it would be her last.

Anna said, 'She gave up after all.'

'Unless something had happened to her.'

'I hope not.'

'Well, she'd tried her best. You can only be ignored for so long.' *And don't I know it.*

Anna twirled a strand of hair around her finger. 'Why would Faye keep these letters when all it would take is one small twist of fate for Edward to find them and realise what she'd done?'

'Perhaps she'd hidden them better than when I found them.' I stretched to counteract the discomfort of sitting for too long. 'The letters make it all more personal, don't they? I mean, the notebook was personal, but it all plays out so tragically in these.'

'Edward never knew how Katherine felt. It's just so sad.' Anna bit her thumbnail, scowling.

'He lost the chance to be a father to Ned.' The thought made me pause and think of my own. Something in the back of my mind shifted.

'We need to be careful, though.' Anna tapped the pen on the pad. 'What if we go digging and Faye sues us or something?'

'I told you, she's dead. The house was all packed up and there's a probate solicitor.'

'Someone might care, though. We can't just invade

people lives. You've broken into Faye's house on the strength of being haunted and marched off with her private things.'

'The door was open.'

'Tell that to the judge.' She was right, of course. 'And for all we know, George might have found Ned.'

'Then why would this be happening to me?'

'We should bear it in mind, though. We can't rule anything out until we have evidence.' She tapped my leg for emphasis.

'So, what do you suggest?'

She skimmed through the information we'd recorded, her brow creased with concentration. Her seriousness was sweet, and I leant in and nuzzled her ear, making her giggle. 'Stop it, silly, I'm thinking.' I gave her peace while I rubbed her back, grateful that she was here and on the case.

'I think there's two strands to follow,' she announced. 'We could try and find where George Locke worked and whether his firm knows the case.'

'David might be able to help with that.'

'Good. And then there's the Public Records Office. We should be able to find some trace of this in there. We might even be able to trace where Ned is now – things must've moved on since Edward's day. And we can confirm that Faye has died. It's not much, but unless you can think of anything better?' I shook my head. 'We just might find something that pings us in the right direction.'

'No harm in trying. I could go there on Monday.'

'A real ghost hunt, isn't it exciting?'

'Yeah, you've not had the shit scared out of you.'

'Where is he now then? Come on, Edward, we want to help you. What's the point of us guessing if you can help us out?'

The notebook slipped off the table and we jumped. We looked at each other and laughed.

'Now look what you've done.' I drew her towards me and kissed her, but she broke off.

'I'd *love* to see a ghost.'

'Trust me, it's overrated.' I kissed her longer and she loosened. As I pushed my tongue into her warm mouth, out of the corner of my eye, I thought I caught a shadow move. Before I could look, Anna rose, blocking my view, and pushed me onto my back.

TWENTY

The weekend with Anna left my ego bursting, but back at work the team wouldn't let me forget my pitiful Friday-night display. Although it was all done in good spirit, behind it was an iron question of my balls.

With Ajay, I could sense the lines blurring. When I pulled on my coat, I knew he'd bristle.

'I'll be out a couple of hours – cover for me.'

'Where are you going?'

'I have an appointment.' I settled on minimal explanation and Ajay didn't answer, his silent judgement prickling me. I looked forward to stamping my authority on the team when I returned; I'd make them sorry for their insults.

I pushed through the Record Office's double doors and swept the place to get my bearings. I faced rows and rows of bookshelves, like a library, except these books were giants. Tall banks of reading tables divided the shelves and I felt like I'd wandered into Lilliput. I'd expected to find a desk, with clerical staff who would answer my queries. Somehow, I had to serve myself.

My face disclosed the challenge, and a white-haired,

mint-scented woman tapped my arm. 'Are you alright, lovey? You look a bit lost. What is it you're after?'

'I'm trying to trace someone. I have a few details…' I pulled my pad from my pocket. 'To be honest, I don't have a clue what I'm doing.'

'Come on, let's have a look.' I showed her the dates I'd noted, along with the details of Ned's birth. She tilted her head to view it through bifocals. 'Is it your family tree? I've been researching mine for three years. It's fascinating, isn't it?'

'Yes, it is.' The ease of the lie pleased me.

'Well, you won't find this American chap here.'

'Oh, really? Why's that?'

'He'll be registered in America.'

'His family are English. Won't there be some way to check?'

'Sorry, lovey, it doesn't work like that. It'll all be held in America.' This wasn't the script. 'But with a bit of patience, I'm sure we'll find the others.'

'Could we look up this death?' I wanted Faye crossed off.

'Yes, we can do that. I'm Jean, by the way.'

'Peter.'

'My son-in-law is called Peter. Lovely lad.'

Feeling grateful that Peter wasn't terrible, I followed Jean to the relevant aisles. She explained how the records were organised and showed me how to search. Once I understood, I looked for Faye's death, while Jean continued her own research, keeping a motherly eye.

Given the state of Dawson Road, I looked backwards from the most recent entries. There were four registers for every year, divided into March, June, September and December. It meant combing through a fair few of the weighty volumes and proved to be a hardy muscle workout. While I tumbled over the pages, the old woman juggled the books with ease, making it look like she was flicking through the *Radio Times*. After trawling back ten years, I'd only found a Daniel Featherstone, who'd died in the area in 1982, and apart from that, I'd found no other candidates.

I tapped at my pad for inspiration and decided to move on to her marriage. Jean showed me the section and I immediately struck gold, finding Edward and Faye in the first book. Seeing their black-inked names sent a rush through my chest.

Spurred on, I wanted to confirm Edward's suicide and went back across to the deaths. Sure enough, there he was in March 1938. The cause of death wasn't listed, but the timing was spot on. I then worked forwards from 1938, trying again to find Faye. I worked right back to where I'd left off and still found no trace. I sighed and rubbed my eyes.

'What's wrong?' Jean had noticed.

'I really thought I'd find this death.'

'Let me see.' Jean peered at my pad. 'Could she have remarried?'

'Ah, yes…'

'Oh, actually, your notes say this year.'

'I'm not sure. I think it's quite recent.'

'I'm just thinking… if she's only just died, those records aren't here yet.'

'Yes, of course. I'm such an idiot.'

'You're new to it, that's all. You had other things to think about.'

'That does make sense, though.' That had to be it because the bank statement on the desk had been in the name of Featherstone.

'You'll need to wait a couple of months, I think.' She patted my arm and I glanced at her watch.

'Crikey, I need to go.'

'Yes, time flies in here.' She checked her watch herself and nodded at her wisdom.

'Thank you so much. I couldn't have managed without you.'

'Hopefully, I'll see you again.'

Jean watched me pack up my pad and when I neared the exit we waved.

I intended to call Anna straight away, but when I walked into the office, Ajay pounced.

'Where the hell have you been? I've been run ragged. Look, mate, I'm all for helping you out, but now you're taking the piss. You'd arranged a call with Mike Anderson, and it was right in the middle of a deal. This is all one-way. I might have lost a pile thanks to you.'

'Shit, I forgot.'

'Yeah, man, you're losing it. You're not taking me down with you.' Ajay stormed off.

I could see the team avoiding my gaze and fury swelled. I waited for just one of them to smirk or crack a smart remark, but they knew better. Nevertheless, I picked on the most respected of their ranks to show them I meant business.

'Helen, meet me in my office at six. I want to go through your accounts.'

She looked at me with a flicker of anger, then caught herself and muttered, 'Okay.'

'Good. Time to spring clean the team.' I marched into my room and slammed the door.

On the other side I crumpled. No matter what I did, it was wrong. And, by picking on Helen, I'd further damaged my cause. Defeated, I called Anna, but she was about to give a presentation and could only spare a few seconds. She agreed to come over to mine later.

By the time Anna arrived, I was on my second whisky. The meeting with Helen had been a slog and I'd just wanted to get out of the place, but after the fuss I'd made, I could hardly cut corners. Now my head pounded, and Anna was a welcome relief. I poured two glasses of red wine and brought her up to speed on the day's detecting.

'So, are we any further forward?' She rubbed my thigh with her hand.

'It doesn't feel like it. I've only confirmed what we already knew and found absolutely nothing on Ned. And I'm still only ninety-nine per cent sure that Faye can't sue us.'

'At least we know that we can trust the notebook.' She took a swig of wine. 'And we have the information in the letters, including an address. Perhaps it's time to track down George.'

'I can imagine what David will make of all this.' I remembered the spooky event we'd shared at New Year and his refusal to acknowledge it.

'Don't tell him. Make something up. You're getting good at that.'

'You, lady, are a bad influence.' I lifted her chin and kissed her. 'A very, very bad influence.' I unbuttoned her blouse.

'Let me be bad in your bed. This sofa nearly killed me last night.' She stood and tugged me by the hand.

Curled around Anna's warm body, I fell into a deep, dreamy sleep. I was in a library, reaching up to the top shelf for a book. I pulled it down and it dropped onto the floor. Then someone was shaking my shoulder...

'Peter! Peter!'

I turned to get another book.

'Peter! Wake up.' Anna shook me again.

'What?'

'Wake up! I can hear something.'

In my stupor, I listened, but my ears were all fog.

'What *is* that?' she said.

My heart went cold. Now I could hear it. It was the scraping sound.

'Shit, not again.' I darted out of bed, grabbed my robe and stepped over to the door. I listened to the tidal swoosh of the noise, trying to get a handle on where it was. There was a sweep, sweep, and I held my breath for the third.

Something smashed against the door.

'Peter!' Anna switched on the lamp.

I held my hand out at Anna. 'Stay there.' And for a moment there was silence. Then footsteps marched towards us, stamp, stamp, stamp, and the knob rattled and turned. I grasped it to stop it from twisting, but it was too strong and curled in my hand. I put my bare foot against the edge of the door, trying to wedge it. The door banged, and a twang of pain stabbed through to the bone. A sickening crack sounded, more like a spine than the wood of the door, and I waited, terrified, for the fiend to break through.

But there was silence.

I raised my trembling hand to the doorknob again and turned to look at Anna. She nodded, so I peeled it half-way.

A mass of blackness met me, which I vanquished with a click of the light. There was no sign of an intruder, and when I checked the door, it looked whole. I felt the grain with my fingertips and found the wood smooth and unbroken.

I took another look at Anna for courage and then crept towards the lounge. Everything looked normal, and as I scanned to make sure, Anna came behind, pressing her body into mine.

'It's okay,' I said. She'd brought a gentle scent of roses, like the liners in Mum's chest of drawers. I turned to reassure her.

She wasn't there.

Before I could make sense of it, a cry came from the bedroom. I sprinted to Anna.

'Someone slapped me.' She was bordering on hysterical.

'What?!'

'It attacked me! It attacked me, look!' A red mark showed on her upper arm.

'Bloody hell.' I drew her close and soothed her with gentle shushes and kisses. It took five minutes for her to settle from panic to distressed calm. When the heat of our bodies was lost to cold air, I tugged the covers around us.

'Is that what happened before?' she asked.

'Things like that have happened.' *But this was far worse.*

'I don't know how you stand it.'

'I told you it gets shit-scary.' I'd earned her respect. 'So much for Father Ryan.'

'You should demand a refund.' She laughed a dry laugh. 'Let's leave the lamp on. I know it's silly, but it feels safer somehow.' She pulled my hand across her body, snuggling into me. We lay, our breathing in harmony, and I could feel her searching for signs.

'Peter, can you smell roses?'

'Shush, go to sleep.'

Not long after that, she did, leaving me behind with her gentle, gaspy snores. I lay there, wide awake, worrying. If Edward wanted our help, what the hell was going on?

TWENTY-ONE

I arranged to meet my brother at The Swan, near his office on Chancery Lane. I arrived first and found a table in the corner of the wooden-panelled walls, underneath a faded print of Horatio Nelson in his full naval regalia. I sat down on the red, upholstered bench seat and placed my pint dead centre on one of the beermats.

David was late, of course, no doubt wrapping up an epic victory, but that gave me time to rehearse. The door burst open and, like a cowboy squaring for the fight, he marched through, followed by Lucy. It hadn't occurred to me that Lucy would join us, and I wondered what she might think.

'Sorry I'm late. Lucy took ages.' He winked.

Lucy tutted with her eyes. 'Lovely to see you, Peter.' She planted a kiss on my cheek.

'Same again?' David nodded at my pint.

'Please.'

Lucy said, 'I wasn't sure if it was a man-to-man talk. I hope you don't mind me joining you?' She unwrapped her coat and draped it over the end of the bench seat.

'Of course not, you might be able to help.'

'Make him behave, you mean.'

David came back balancing a triangle of drinks in his hands and four packets of crisps under his arms. He dumped it all down in the middle of the table. I set the drinks on beermats while Lucy ripped open the crisps, laying them out for us all to dip in.

'So, what's all this about? Finally been caught money laundering?' He took a deep swig of his pint and a quarter of it disappeared. I noticed no '*How have you been?*'.

'I just wanted to check something with you.'

'Well, let's get the business out of the way.'

'It's nothing difficult, I hope. I'm trying to help a friend and said I'd have a word with you.' David didn't even try to look interested as he wiped his nose to catch the runs from the change of temperature. 'He's hitting a dead end with some legal stuff.'

'Go on then.'

'His aunt died recently, and there's some money tied up in it. He needs to trace other relatives because there's a fund. And he's not sure how that all works.'

'Oh yeah.' This was obviously beneath him.

I took them through a sober version of events, outlining a family who'd lost touch with distant relatives in America. I shared the scandal of the long-ago secret pregnancy and how my friend needed to find that grown-up relative to settle the estate. While David waited for me to cut to the chase and come out with what I wanted, Lucy asked lots of questions. An analysis of my story wasn't the plan and I had to make up answers on the spot – Anna was right, I was getting good at it. Then I tied myself into a knot.

'Sorry, I'm confused.' Lucy would unravel me sooner or later. 'A solicitor is already involved. So why does your friend need David's help?'

'A solicitor was searching, years ago. The point is, my friend either needs to find that solicitor, or—'

'Why did they search for him years ago? Hasn't the aunt just died?'

'Do you know the solicitor's name?' David cut in, unwittingly saving me.

'George Locke.'

'Of Locke and Noble?'

'I've no idea.'

'Probably is. And if it is George Locke of Locke and Noble, it'll be costing a fortune.' It never occurred to me that there might be a cost and that prospect wasn't appealing. 'It's your lucky day because I went to uni with James Locke.'

Lucy said, 'What a coincidence.'

'Yes and no. It's a big family. It's hard not to run into them. And all children born to Messrs Locke and Noble are working away in that firm.' Yep, that was a dig. 'I haven't spoken to James for a while, but I could give him a ring.'

'Well… yes… thank you.' It *was* an incredible coincidence and felt a little too close to home. Remembering my information was built on stolen documents, worry twinged in my chest.

'If he recognises the name George, I'll pass on your number and you can fill him in.'

'Yes, that sounds good.' I nodded, convincing myself it would all work out fine.

'What you been up to then?' David moved on.

'I'm seeing Anna again. You remember Anna, we went out at uni.'

'No, I don't think so.' Of course he didn't. 'Oh, before I forget, Sarah wants you to call her.'

'David, don't be rude,' said Lucy. 'Go on, Peter, tell us about Anna.'

'It's okay, I'm used to him. What did Sarah want?'

'Something about Michael.'

'Michael?'

'Yes. I can't remember what it was.' He didn't make any effort to either. 'You need to give her a ring.'

Before I had a chance to push it, David waved his empty glass. I bought another round and then David started talking about his new car, a BMW something or other. It was my turn to be bored, while he and Lucy rabbited on about leather seats and sunroofs. The rest of the evening passed in a similar way, with David claiming most of the oxygen to impress us with his latest endeavours. As we all had work in the morning, we reined in our drinking and called it a night around nine.

David surpassed my expectations as I got a call at work the very next day.

'Hello, Peter. My name is James Locke. David asked me to give you a ring.'

'James, thank you for calling. Did David explain what it's about?'

'He didn't say much. He asked me to call.'

Typical David. I repeated the story of my friend's search, hoping it sounded credible.

'Well, as you will know, the case was long before my time. Let me dig around and see what I can find.'

'Thank you, I really appreciate it.'

'And failing that, I can always ask George.'

'Really?' A million thoughts raced through my head.

'Sure, he loves it when us youngsters defer to him.'

'I didn't think he'd still be around.' I realised how awful that sounded. 'I mean, it was a long time ago.'

'Oh, he's definitely still around.' James laughed. 'I'll give you a call next week and let you know what I've found.'

I put down the phone, feeling hopeful. It was less than an hour when he rang again.

'Peter, you won't believe this. After I came off the phone, my great-grandfather dropped in. Looks like you're onto a winner. Can you call by to see me next week?'

'Erm… next week? Yes, I think so. Is there anything you can share now?'

'I don't even know myself yet. He's promised to fill me in later.'

'Okay…' I checked my diary. 'How about Monday, around two?'

'Two-fifteen works for me.'

'Great, see you then.'

I sat in a trance of thought. I needed to know where all this was leading – how on earth could I wait until Monday?

I ended the working day by going through Dan's accounts. It was a better-spirited meeting than Helen's. He enjoyed my interest and didn't mind taking ideas from a deteriorating genius. We finished around seven, and I was just packing up when I remembered to call Sarah. I sat back down and dialled.

'You've spoken to David then,' said Sarah.

'Yes, but he didn't tell me anything.'

'Bloody David. Are you okay?'

'Yes, thanks, you?'

'Are you sure?'

'Of course, why?'

'It's Michael. He's convinced that something has happened to you. He's having nightmares and waking up screaming. I keep telling him that you're okay, but he's getting worse.'

'Why would Michael think that?'

'I've no idea. I hoped you might know. I'm at my wits' end. Adam is hardly sleeping – he's like a zombie.'

'What are you going to do?'

'I think Michael needs to see you, to see with his own eyes that you're alright. I know how busy you are, so I'm not asking you to come up. I was thinking of bringing him to London. I could stay with David and show Michael around. He'd love that.' Now I knew why David had 'forgotten'; it was all too weird for him.

'Good idea. It would be great to see you both anyway.'

'I'm thinking of coming a week on Friday. I'll confirm when I know for sure.'

I slotted the phone into the receiver with a now-familiar sense of dread. This wasn't Sarah. Sarah was practical, down-to-earth, the one who mended everything. This had to be bad.

TWENTY-TWO

With emotions ranging from excitement, impatience and panic, I negotiated my way through to Monday. At half-one, I prepared to slip off. I'd overspent on loyalty, so I played on the team's unscrupulous dynamic.

'I'm off to meet a new client,' I called across the office, deciding to stay safe with a lie.

Ajay said, 'You know I've got a meeting.'

'It's okay, Helen is picking it up for me.'

With a face of thunder, Ajay collected his jacket and marched off.

I headed up to Holborn and into Lincoln's Inn Fields. I found the prestigious offices of Locke and Noble in a grand, terraced building with a wide, black front door, framed by two white pillars. A polished brass plate on the wall announced, '*Messrs W A Locke & P C F Noble, Est 1843*'.

Once through the oversized door, a cavernous hallway with creaking boards and mellow, creamy polish welcomed me. On my left was a plain oak door marked 'Reception', and behind that, a spacious waiting area opened, where a blonde, ponytailed, young woman sat behind a desk. She looked up and smiled.

'Can I help you, sir?'

'My name is Peter Tyler and I have an appointment to see James Locke.'

She checked a list and nodded to confirm. 'Please take a seat, Mr Locke will be with you shortly.' She gestured towards an empty waiting area in the bay window. I chose the leather two-seater with a view onto the street. Quality shone through every furnishing, an unwelcome reminder that expertise comes at a cost.

I glanced at the magazines arranged neatly on the glass table, and when nothing took my fancy, I settled on watching the view of the square. The park-garden in the centre lay adorned in its winter browns, but the bright, dry day hinted at the hope of spring to come. I watched people passing, scuttling along, deceived by the sun, and hurrying out of the cold into the surrounding buildings. Then I saw a woman in a long, black coat, standing across the street and staring in my direction. I doubted that she could see beyond the window's reflection, yet she stared so directly that I felt she could. A van drove by and I half expected her to disappear, like a cliché of a ghost, but she was still there and still staring. I shifted in my chair and jumped as a hand touched my shoulder.

'Sorry, I did not mean to startle you.' I met the eyes of an old man, who could have been anywhere between eighty and a hundred years old. He was wearing a grey, pinstripe, three-piece suit that looked at least one size too big for his shrinking frame. 'My name is George Locke and I believe that you are Peter Tyler?'

'Yes.' I was staggered to meet the very man himself.

'I told James that I would meet with you today. I hope you don't mind?' He reached out a gnarled, liver-spotted hand and softly shook mine.

'No, of course not. It's an honour.'

'I'm not so sure of that.' He chuckled. 'Please, come with me.'

I followed as he ambled out of reception and continued down the corridor to another oak door. He opened it onto an office lined with fabulous old bookcases that reached to the ceiling. A mahogany desk stood proud in the corner and two maroon-leather, high-back, winged Chesterfields framed the fireplace, where a healthy fire crackled with coal. Mr Locke helped take off my overcoat and, after hanging it on the stand, ushered me towards the chairs.

'I thought it would be easier to speak with you myself.' He bent and dropped into the opposite chair. 'When my great-grandson told me about your enquiry, I must admit, it gave me a shock. I could not believe that someone was interested in Katherine Bell, after all this time. And I am very curious to find out who you are.' He eyeballed me, my bowels squirmed and then he continued.

'I was a friend of Edward Featherstone and worked on this case myself, as a private favour.' I nodded to show I was following. 'It was not a case that other people knew about. I had to be discreet because... well, let's just say that matters were delicate, and I did not want the attention of certain people.'

'Like her father?'

The old man glared back at me. I'd offered my suggestion to show that I understood the sensitivities, but Mr Locke grew instantly wary.

'Before I go on, can you tell me what interest you have in this?' Mr Locke's earnest, grey eyes drilled into me, and I knew this was it. I'd practised my new story a dozen times; however, facing such an intimate situation with this sincere gentleman, I could find no confidence in lying. He waited, still nodding, and, wondering at my own madness, I realised that I was going to tell him the whole crazy story.

I cleared my throat and was just about to speak when he raised his hand to stop me.

'Aha.' With the difficulty of old age, he levered himself out of his chair and walked over to a table in the corner, where a crystal decanter and glasses rested. He poured two large whiskies and passed a glass into my hand. Once he'd settled again, I felt his permission to continue.

I drew in a deep breath and started on my tale. I told him everything that had happened since taking the book. I described the strange happenings and the need to go to Edward's house. I shared finding the letters and Edward's notebook and how that had led to a trip to the Records Office. And finally, I explained that my brother had pointed me towards James and the very offices that we were sitting in that afternoon. As I relived the whole journey, the weight of it drained away.

When I'd finished, I sat back and expected to see scepticism. However, Mr Locke's body language showed something else, and after a few moments of silence, he spoke.

'You have been most open with me, and I am extremely glad that you felt able to share your experience. And given the, let's say, supernatural nature of your story, I thank you for trusting me with all the remarkable details.' He stared solidly into my eyes, and I had no doubt that he believed every word. 'I was indeed involved in Edward's business. And to confirm your thinking, I have been totally unsuccessful in tracing his son. Some friend I am, eh?

'I think about him almost every day, especially now that I have too much time on my hands and not enough to occupy my mind. I have lived a good life, full of children and... I have been most lucky. But for Edward things were different. He was so angry and unhappy when he died. It's not a way to go.

'We met at our gentleman's club and hit it off straight away, as they say. It was our interest in politics that drew us together, and our shared passion for a good debate. I was a keen supporter of his political career and over the years, we became very close.

'I know that when he married Faye, her family were in uproar. They were extremely rich, and in their opinion, their jewel had married way beneath herself. Edward was a real charmer, a devilishly good-looking man, who turned every lady's eye. Faye fell hopelessly in love with him, and for a long time they were happy.

'However, they tried for years to have children and unfortunately, it never happened. Faye could not come to terms with it, poor thing. But as you know, she threw herself into other interests and became a well-respected figure in the community. She loved gardening and helped convert waste ground around London into flourishing play areas. And her father was a patron of the Shrewsbury Theatre, where she put on several shows with her under-privileged drama students. Faye won a number of awards, and in fact, yes, I remember now, the theatre even commissioned a portrait in her honour.' Mr Locke paused to take a drink.

'Yes, Edward and Faye were content enough. But when Edward met Katherine, he fell head over heels. She was beautiful, playful and extremely enigmatic. Her gorgeous blue eyes, long blonde hair and radiant smile melted all men's hearts. I must admit, I very much admired her myself!' He chuckled. 'And Edward had lost none of his charisma. So, despite the age gap, they began an affair, with no care about the consequences.

'He was devastated… no, *destroyed* when she left, and went out of his mind trying to find her.

'Then Edward's father came into a substantial sum of money. His shares in a textiles company paid off greatly just before his death and Edward was the sole inheritor. Edward never told Faye about the money because he wanted to leave it to Ned. As things stood, with the boy not recognised in law as his son, he worried that Faye might claim everything.' Mr Locke eyed me to check I was following him and, satisfied, carried on.

'I know that I did too much for Edward, but I am sure he would have done the same for me. I helped him set up a trust fund for Ned, stipulating that if we could not find him forty years after Edward's death, the money would go to charity. Due to the sensitive and, you might say, controversial nature of the case, I dealt with everything personally. No one else knew the full story, and that was the way I intended to keep it.

'During what became Edward's final months, with him steeped in depression, Faye was forced to take control of their circumstances. Rather than come to me, she transferred their affairs to her father's solicitor. That was fortunate because I was then able to avoid the conflict of interest.

'I searched and searched for Katherine and the boy but got nowhere. I guessed that she had changed her name and although I found and followed all sorts of leads, it was like trying to find a needle in a haystack. I did track down her cousin in New York – and you will not believe this. I found out that on the very day I wrote to her, she was run down by a cab and killed.' He gave a shake of his head. 'So, by the time of Edward's death, apart from ruling options out, we were no further forward.'

'And how did he die?'

'Do you not know? He took his own life.'

'I thought so – I wasn't sure.'

'Oh, it was dreadful. He jumped out of his bedroom window, and thankfully, Mrs Talbert and not Faye found him.'

'Mrs Talbert?'

'The housekeeper. I don't know why he made it so... gruesome. And why he left it to chance. I mean, he could have survived a fall like that and lived the rest of his life like a vegetable. Thankfully, he broke his neck and was killed outright.'

'He must have been desperate.'

'Yes.'

'And you never found Ned.'

'No. I promised Edward that I would keep searching, but it seemed that, true to her word, Katherine had disappeared. It is very upsetting to find out that Faye had stolen her letters.'

Mr Locke broke off and stared into the fire.

'And why do you think Edward has made contact now, through me? As far as I know, I have no connection to him or Katherine.'

'Perhaps you are sensitive to these things.' I shook the idea out of my head. 'What I do know is that the forty years is up next year. There is little time left and I imagine Edward, God rest his soul, is determined to see that Ned receives what is rightfully his. And he is doing everything in his power to achieve that.'

'Even from beyond the grave.' As I said it, the words sent goosepimples down my spine. 'Do you really believe that?'

'Yes, I actually do.' I looked at him for more. 'Edward called me at the office one afternoon, to check what instructions were in place in the event of his death. Even though we had been through those arrangements several times, he was anxious to hear that I understood. Like the dumb fool I was, it did not strike me as odd at the time. We spoke for a few minutes, and I was pleased at how chipper he sounded; he was like his old cheerful self. But once he felt satisfied that everything was in place, he hung up, without so much as a goodbye.

'A couple of mornings later, I sat reading my newspaper at breakfast and nearly choked on my toast. There, in the obituary column, was the announcement of Edward's death. At first, the only thing that struck me was the shock of losing him when he seemed quite well. And then I noticed the date of his passing. It was the day before our phone call.' Mr Locke peered at my reaction. 'Of course, I knew it to be a printing mistake. However, when I checked, the date was indeed correct.

'Now, I'm not a man ever taken by fancy. I know with absolute certainty that I spoke with Edward the day *after* he had departed this life. Despite trying, I have never found a rational explanation for it, but I am damn sure that it happened.'

With those last words, we both sat staring into the fire. George tried to take a drink from his empty glass and then put it down on the side table. I watched him a little while longer and then broke the silence.

'What will happen to the house now that both Faye and Edward are dead?'

'Faye had two brothers, so there is likely to be someone on her side who is set to inherit whatever there is. Although, from what I heard, Faye had a complete breakdown after Edward's death. It was as if she had died herself. As I understand it, she refused to see any of her family and lived

138

as a recluse. So, whoever inherits, it will be a gift from a stranger.'

We sat in silence for a few more moments, digesting each other's stories.

'I must get back to the office.' We'd been talking for almost an hour and a half.

'Of course, you must.' He glanced at his watch, raised his eyebrows and turned back to me. 'I cannot convey in words how glad I am that you came here today. And I cannot believe that I have another chance to help my poor friend Edward. Oh, and on that, did you bring anything with you to help us trace Ned?'

'Yes, good point. I brought the letters and the notebook.'

I fetched my coat from the stand and handed them over. Mr Locke puffed up like a man receiving a great prize.

'And, forgive me for asking, was there any other paperwork of interest?'

'Not that I saw. But actually, my search was cut short.'

'Oh?'

'There was someone else in the house. They seemed to be hiding upstairs.' George stared. 'Like I said, the door was open when I got there, and I didn't think much of it at first. Someone had obviously broken in, but it never occurred to me that they were still in there. When I heard noises, I got out of there quick, but a man knocked me over as he ran for the door.'

'Did you see what he looked like?'

'No, it was dark.'

'Sounds like you had a lucky escape.' He nodded his head in sympathy and then looked down at his lap. He picked up the notebook and pointed it at me. 'I will ask James to get on with this immediately and let you know what we find.' Then he eased forward in his chair, making it obvious that he intended to remain seated. 'It was very nice to meet you, Peter. Thank you so much for bringing this here. Would you be so kind as to find your own way out?'

We shook hands and then I left, delighted with the afternoon's progress.

TWENTY-THREE

Sarah came down that Friday as promised, and I arranged to go over with Anna on Saturday morning. On the phone, I could sense Sarah's uncertainty about Anna – she wanted family time – but as Lucy was there, I couldn't see the issue.

I met up with Anna at King's Cross, where we caught the Circle Line to Sloane Square. David's Chelsea flat was a short walk from the station, in one of the trendier areas of London. Like mine, the block had originally been a single residence and was now split into several exclusive apartments. I pressed the intercom and David buzzed us into the black and white tiled lobby. As we made our way up the stairs, I could see that Anna approved before she'd even seen the flat.

We knocked and Lucy opened the door. 'Hi, come in.' We walked into the brightly lit hallway.

'Lucy, this is Anna.'

'Hi, Anna, lovely to meet you.' She smiled a generous greeting.

'Nice to meet you too.'

'Let me take your coats.'

We handed them over and followed Lucy into the sleek, lilac and white-toned lounge. Original watercolours adorned the walls, and ceramic ornaments, vases and lamps showed off Lucy's artistic flair. David, Sarah and Michael sat spread over two deep-cushioned, black-fabric sofas.

'This is Anna.' I swept my hand out to present her.

'Hi, Anna, I'm David. The good-looking one.'

Lucy rolled her eyes. 'Ignore him, we do.'

'Nice flat,' said Anna. 'I love this area.'

'We'll be selling soon, if you're interested.' David loved an opportunity.

'Selling, why?'

'She's forcing me to marry her and demanding a house.'

'Oh, that's lovely, congratulations.' She smiled over to Lucy.

'Don't mind me.' Sarah stood up for attention.

I said, 'Sarah, come here,' and we hugged. 'You remember Anna.'

'Yes, hi. Michael, say hello.'

For the first time, I registered Michael and understood Sarah's concern. He was a different boy to my Christmas playmate. He stared with no joy, his face flat, his skin pallid with dark rings circling his eyes. He didn't move from Sarah's side.

'Look, Michael, Uncle Peter has come to see you. Are you going to say hello?' Sarah had her jolly voice on, but the strain was clear.

Michael looked up at me. 'Hello, Uncle Peter.'

'What's all this I've been hearing about you?' I squatted down to his level.

'Nothing.'

'Your mum says you've been worried about me.'

'No.' He shrank away, burying his face into Sarah's side.

'Ah,' Anna said, 'he's shy, bless him.'

'Michael, don't be silly. It's only Uncle Peter,' said Sarah.

'He'll come round when he's ready,' Anna added, matter-of-fact, but Sarah looked irritated.

'Who's for a drink?' Lucy broke the exchange.

We placed orders for teas and coffees and settled down on the sofas. Sarah told us about Michael's newly decorated bedroom, and we exaggerated our excitement. She tried to get him talking about school, but he stayed subdued and quiet. Sarah chatted on with nervous energy, promising Michael a trip to the zoo and a ride on a tour bus. Lucy wanted Sarah's help with buying wedding shoes, so Sarah asked David to take Michael to the cinema while they shopped. It started to feel like Anna and I had crashed a private party. I lasted an hour and a half before I'd had enough.

'I'm going to make a move, I have a meeting this afternoon.' I stood to go, nodding at Anna.

'Really?' That caught Sarah's attention.

Anna put her arm around me. 'He works too h—'

'Will you make it to the zoo?' Sarah cut in.

'Yes, of course.' I looked at Michael. 'I'm going to show you how to feed the penguins.' For the first time, I'd raised Michael's smile. 'And then we're going to hunt tigers.'

Michael looked at Sarah. 'And lions?'

'Yes, my love.' Sarah smiled. 'Lots of lions.'

Lucy handed back our coats, and when we hit the street, Anna took my arm. 'Was it my imagination or was your sister a bit funny with me?'

'She's just stressed about Michael.'

'I'll give tomorrow a miss.'

'No, don't do that. I'm sure you're welcome.' I pulled her close as we walked. 'Besides, I need you to protect me from the ferocious beasts,' I growled, and nuzzled her hair.

'They're your family.'

'Oh, very funny.' I squeezed her into me and kissed her through her giggles.

As Anna lived near the zoo, I stayed at hers that night. Her flat sat top centre in a crescent of smart apartments. Her lounge looked pristine, with cream sofas, rugs, curtains, cabinets and even cream candles. My being there made it untidy. Anna rustled up curry from her well-stocked fridge and we spent the evening watching TV.

In the weak morning sunshine, we strolled across to Regent's Park, arm in arm like long-term lovers. We found everyone at the zoo's entrance, buttoned up for a January day.

Sarah saw me studying Michael. 'He slept through, the first time in two weeks.' She brushed his fringe with her fingertips. 'It must have done him the world of good seeing you.'

I smiled at Michael, and he dropped his eyes to the floor. 'I can't wait to get started on our animal hunt,' I said, and he looked back up at me with a hint of a grin.

David and Lucy wandered towards the café, leaving Sarah, Michael, Anna and I studying the map. The excitement was too much for Michael to contain and he burst out a long list of animals he wanted to see. The lions were his number-one priority, but they were on the furthest side. He had a healthy dose of the sulks when Sarah said he must wait.

We started at the aquarium and followed Sarah's systematic route round. It didn't take long for Michael's interest in everything to outweigh his troubles. He ran back and forth, tugging at my arm every two minutes to show me his discoveries. Seeing Michael enjoying himself, Sarah relaxed, her smiles reaching the corners of her mouth as she thawed and chatted to Anna.

'Over here, Uncle Peter. Look! A monkey.'

'That's a gorilla.'

He ran over and waved as the animal paced up and down its territory. 'He looks scary.'

'Do you think that's King Kong?'

He looked hard at me. '*Lions* are the king of the jungle.'

'Most lions don't live in jungles.' I ruffled his hair.

'Where do they live?'

'On plains.'

'Oh.' He looked confused for a moment.

'African plains. Wide areas, not aeroplanes.'

That cleared things up for him and he turned back to watch the gorilla.

'Uncle Peter.'

'Yes?' I looked down at him, smiling, and saw seriousness clouding his face.

'Who's Edward?'

The smile froze on my lips.

'Michael! Michael!' Sarah shouted. 'Come and look, there's a baby gorilla playing.'

He ran over to Sarah, leaving me dumbfounded.

'You look like you've seen a ghost.' Anna put her arm through mine.

'I have.'

'Eh?'

I checked that Sarah was out of earshot. 'Michael… he knows about Edward.'

'What?'

'He's just asked me who Edward is.'

'Oh my goodness. How? What did you say?'

'Nothing. Sarah called him away.'

'You need to talk to him.'

'I know. I'll try and get him on his own again.'

'Bloody hell. This is so creepy.'

Conspiring with Anna, I tried to manoeuvre chances to chat to Michael, but each time Sarah was close on our heels, keen to be part of his fun. Lucy and David called it a day early on, arranging to meet Sarah back at the flat. The afternoon was darkening, bringing with it a sharp breeze, and around three, Sarah suggested a coffee. Resigning myself to defeat, I led the way to the café.

Sarah and Anna chatted as I brought over the drinks.

'What are you doing this evening?' Sarah asked.

'We have no plans,' I said.

'Join us for dinner then. We're going out for pizza. It was Michael's choice, sorry.' She winked at Michael.

'That would be great, thank you,' said Anna.

Then Michael spoke. 'I told Uncle Peter about Edward.'

'Okay, darling.' Sarah was only half listening.

'Oh yes, Edward.' Anna eyes pooled wide and I cringed.

'What?' Sarah looked back and forth at us both. 'You know who he means?'

I gave Anna a pointed look to silence her. 'No, it's—'

'Yes, you do!'

I shook my head. I didn't want to explain things on the hoof.

'Peter! Tell me!' Sarah's face said I had no choice.

'We've been trying to… we've…'

'We've been trying to trace someone,' Anna helped. 'It's… unusual. It's unusual because the people involved… are… not around.'

'What *is* she talking about?' Sarah stared at me.

'Look, Sarah, I'm sure this is a coincidence. A book came into my possession. It led me into something. And ever since, I've been having weird experiences.'

'What experiences?'

'Like… being haunted.'

'Don't you dare!' People on other tables turned to look. 'Don't you dare start this again. Whatever *she* has got you doing—'

'That's really not fair—' said Anna.

'…keep it away from my son. I brought him here because I need your help, and you're telling him this? You know how worried I am. I need more from you, Peter. I need you to step up for once.'

Michael started to cry.

'Sarah, I'm sorry. I *am* trying to help.' *Please calm down and listen!* 'I think Michael knows something that we need—'

'It's all about what you need now, is it? Michael, don't cry, darling, it's okay.' She hugged him and stroked his hair.

'If Michael knows something, shouldn't we talk about it?'

'I should've known that you were behind this. You even had the nerve to act like nothing was going on! I don't know what you've been filling his head with, but it has to stop.'

'I'm not doing anything, I swear.'

'Really? We should go.' She started wrapping Michael's coat around him.

Anna tried, 'Come on, Sarah.'

'*You* have no idea about this family.'

'Peter isn't trying to hurt Michael.'

Sarah carried on fastening Michael's coat.

I said, 'We'll still join you later.'

'No! Sorry, but given what you're up to, I don't think you should.'

'This isn't a way to say goodbye. Look, Michael's upset.' I couldn't let them go back to Norfolk like this.

'Don't *you* tell *me* about my own son!'

147

'I only mean… let him see that I'm okay.'

'Are you? Are you okay, Peter? You lose your promotion.' I felt Anna's eyes on me – that was news to her. 'You're going out with her after she's wrecked your life once. And now you're being haunted. Whatever is going on for you, get it sorted, but leave my son out of it!' She snatched her things together. 'Michael, come on.'

'Can we still go to the shop?' His eyes pleaded.

'Yes. Say goodbye to Uncle Peter and… Anna.'

Sarah didn't meet my eye as Michael picked up his zoo map and gloves, and then hugged Anna and I goodbye.

'Sorry, Uncle Peter,' he whispered into my ear.

'Don't you worry.' I gave him a wink and he tried to smile.

Without looking at us, Sarah said a brusque goodbye and ushered Michael towards the shop. I didn't have the skill to retrieve the situation.

Anna said, 'I'm sorry. I just didn't know what to say. I've really messed things up for you.'

'No, you haven't.' I put on my coat, and we moved to leave. 'I didn't know what to say either. She'll be okay.' I didn't really believe that; I'd never seen Sarah so angry. I was smarting inside.

'How could he know about Edward?' Anna took my hand as we walked out into rain.

'I've no idea. I wish we could ask him.'

'This is amazing.'

'What? I'm glad you think so.'

'No, sorry. I mean the fact that Michael can tune into this. You've never discussed it with him?'

'I've never said a word to him or Sarah about the book and…' I stopped.

'What?'

'The priest warned me. Of course, yes. I can't believe I forgot.' I replayed the conversation I'd had with Father Boyle at Christmas.

'Michael sees it too? Well, that's it! Somehow, he's tuning into this. He's picking up on what's happening to you. Maybe he knows more than we do. This is important. We need to speak to him.'

'Are we on the same planet? You saw Sarah's reaction.'

'Work on it, she'll come round. This is so exciting.'

At least someone in this catastrophe was happy.

TWENTY-FOUR

The Wednesday after our zoo visit, Sarah called me at work.

'Sarah, I'm so pleased you've—'

'Peter! You need to tell me what's going on. I can't stop thinking about it and I'm getting angrier and angrier.'

My blood pressure peaked. 'I really don't know what to say.'

'Tell me everything. I'll listen this time.'

I told Sarah an edited version of events, missing out anything that might have sent her off the scale – I'd found an old book with a message inside, a message asking for help to find a long-lost son and reunite him with a fortune. I'd been curious and followed it up. Instead of explaining about the house, I said that details of the solicitor were written on the card and David had put me in touch with him.

'So how is Michael involved in this? Did you tell him about it at Christmas?'

'Well, that's the weird thing, I didn't know any of this at Christmas.'

She took a deep breath. 'You expect me to believe that? You expect me to believe that you're involved in some dead person's shit and that my five-year-old son is having nightmares by coincidence?'

'I didn't say that, Sarah. There's obviously more to it, but I didn't know at Christmas.'

The line went silent for a few long seconds.

'Why are you lying, Peter?' She tried to control her voice. 'I spoke to Reverend Boyle yesterday. He's noticed the change in Michael and called round to see if everything was okay. He said that he warned you about this at Christmas!'

'No, that's not what happened—'

'So Reverend Boyle is a liar now, is he?'

'I don't mean that – it's just not what he said.'

'I saw you talking to him. I even asked you what it was about.'

'Honestly, Sarah, I had no idea what he was on about. Neither did you.'

'Don't you dare bring me into this. If I'd had any idea that Michael was being drawn into something, do you think I'd have ignored it?'

'No—'

'I wanted an open conversation with you. Help me understand.' Tears choked her words. 'Michael is *ill*, and whatever you and that woman are doing, *just stop it!*'

'I have stopped. I've already handed it over to the solicitor.'

'And how do we help Michael?'

'I don't know,' I sighed, and thought for a moment. 'What about Father Boyle?'

'Oh, Father Boyle has the answers now, does he?'

'I don't know what else to suggest.'

'No, I can see that. I'm *so* angry that you put some stranger's business before your own nephew's health. You never gave him a thought.'

'That's unfair.'

'I feel so upset with you, Peter. I need to go.' She hung up. I sat floored, the wind knocked out of me.

Ajay bounced in. 'Hey, boss, you missed the—'

'Get out!'

Then Philip walked in behind him.

'What the hell?' He stared at me like I was a lunatic. 'Ajay's got good news. I've had a call from Robert.' The lead partner. *So Ajay gets the news before me now.* 'We've smashed our targets.'

'Look, sorry. That last call was difficult.'

'Yes, it's getting more and more difficult for you. We're going out for a drink, but I guess you're not such good company. Come on, Ajay, leave him to it.'

They walked out together, leaving my door wide open. I watched them collect several others and noted how familiar Ajay was with Philip. I was already far from their thoughts.

Everything was slipping away.

I rolled open my bottom drawer and looked down at a bottle of scotch from Dan at Christmas. Johnnie Walker was waiting to welcome me to a different kind of party, his amber liquid beaming mellow happiness. I took out a dusty glass from the back of the drawer and set it on my desk. Then I twisted open the bottle, the familiar crack of the metal lid already bringing satisfaction. I poured myself a triple, one for each gulp, and then poured another, before calling Anna and arranging to go round.

I'd had more than enough to drink but collected the customary bottle of red on the way. Anna was already drinking when I arrived and handed me a glass from the open bottle. I settled on her plush cream sofa and launched straight into retelling my call with Sarah. By the time I'd finished, Anna was wound up even more than me.

'You'd think she'd give you the benefit of the doubt,' she said.

'No chance. She was so angry.'

'She always is.'

'Don't be like that. She's really worried about Michael.'

'Why would she blame you? Can't she see that this is something unusual?'

'I promised her that it was over.'

'Why?'

'Because it is. James is searching for Ned now.'

'We're not just going to hand it over and forget about it. We need to make sure it all works out. And I want to know what happens, even if you don't.'

'It's not really our business.'

'What are you talking about? If it weren't for us, there'd be no business.'

'I've given my word.'

'You've given your word? So that's it? Thanks for dragging me into this, but you've spoken and that's it?'

'Michael is ill! What sort of people would we be if we carried on?'

'Don't try and make me feel like I'm the unreasonable person here, just because I've got an open mind. He's not ill, he's… he's having some sort of psychic connection. And that's pretty brilliant. Remember how shit-scared you've been – do you think that will just go away?'

'Now that James is involved, yes, I do.'

'Oh, hang on.' She put her glass down on the table. 'Sarah thinks this is all me, doesn't she? She thinks I'm a bad influence. Is that it?'

'No.'

'You're a terrible liar, Peter! I get it now. Big sister doesn't approve, and little brother needs approval. I thought you'd grown up. You've just swapped your dad for your sister.'

'Perhaps I should go – we've both had a long day.'

153

'Yes, you should. I might encourage you to do something like stand on your own two feet, and we couldn't have that. You couldn't even deal with Edward without *me*.'

I travelled home in a fury, riled by Anna's opinions. Of course, I knew she was right, and that annoyed me even more. But she didn't need to speak to me like that, scolding me like I was a child.

As soon as I stepped in, I went straight for the whisky. I poured another and then another, and dared the night terrors to find me. And when even they let me down, I punched the sofa in frustration. I let rip, pummelling the tired upholstery until my arms burned and my knuckles felt tender. And then I collapsed, exhausted. I fell asleep and my mixed-up emotions brought dreams of my father. He was calling out, trying to tell me something.

I woke and something felt familiar. I just couldn't catch its thread.

TWENTY-FIVE

Wakening into my senses, I looked about, confused as to why I was in my chair and not in bed. A pain split my head and my body trembled with the shakes. When I stood up the room whirled, and I lurched for the bathroom, just reaching the toilet bowl in time to vomit a jet of yellow fluid. Then I sank to my knees and the stink of sick brought another heave that cramped my stomach with its violent retch. I wanted to stay there and die, but a full day of work lay in wait.

I shuffled around the flat, alternating vomiting with getting ready, and left for work when it felt safe. The cold air brought minor relief that was lost when I sank into the stuffy underground. I spent the tube ride hypnotising myself not to be sick. I felt grey and sweat streamed through every pore. I couldn't believe how stupid I'd been. Before Edward, I could have gone days without a drink, and now I couldn't stop at four. I made a solemn promise to myself – no more drinking!

I walked into the office late and saw Ajay and Philip chatting and laughing. They'd forged a unified partnership, all mirrored body language and mutual respect. They turned to look at me and I saw their disgust. 'Ah, look, there's Peter Tyler, the man who had everything. Was on the verge of partner... *No!* ...Oh yes, and then he started seeing dead people... *Really?!* ...Couldn't take the pressure and his mind clean snapped... *Geez, what a waste...* Well, his father always said he was a loser.'

I settled down at my desk and fought the urge to throw up, 'Oh no, not here.' I grabbed my bin, but as I stared into the empty void of paper dust and fluff, the feeling passed. I saw people gathering in the main office for the daily meeting and staggered out to join them. I heard nothing but the pounding in my head, and after clinging on until Philip's final words, I retreated to my office.

The phone vibrated through my injured brain, and I grabbed it to cut the noise. It was Anna.

'Peter, I'm sorry for losing my temper last night. I can understand why you're worried about Michael.'

'Thank you.' *And thank goodness.* I wasn't up for a fight.

'And I know we can leave things to James now.'

'Yes.'

'It's just...'

'What?' My head spun.

'Edward has chosen you for this, not the other way around... So even if you try and step away, the weird stuff might continue.'

'We won't know until we try. And anyway, I've been thinking about that, and it's been quiet since I passed everything to George.'

'Well in that case, what's the harm in carrying on?'

'Anna, I promised Sarah. We don't know that Michael is safe from all this.'

'And you're not just saying this because you're scared of her?'

'No, of course not.'

'Okay. You win. I was enjoying the search, but fair enough. Anyway, I want to… Oh, hang on, I need to get the other phone. I'll call you back in a minute.'

At last, there was something good. And now that Anna and I were on the same page, I could try and make things right with Sarah. I resolved to visit Sarah at the weekend, to explain the whole thing. I'd apologise face to face and clear up the misunderstanding with Father Boyle.

The phone rang as promised and I killed it before the second ring. 'Hi—'

'Peter, it's James Locke. I've got some brilliant news! We've managed to trace Ned.'

'What? Oh… that's great.' I hoped that sounded more positive than I felt.

'We followed the trail left in those letters. We traced his phone number, and it's fair to say, he was pretty shocked to hear from us. He still lives in Boston with his wife and two boys, but Katherine died some years ago.'

'Probably when the letters stopped.'

'Yes, probably. It was all very overwhelming for him. He already knew that Edward was his father but thought he wanted nothing to do with him. The idea of an inheritance cheered him up, though.'

'I bet. So, what's the next step?'

'His solicitor is sending over documents for the identity checks.'

'And then it's all done?' *It's all over.*

'More or less, after I've drawn up the paperwork to transfer the inheritance. And I think Ned will come over here to complete it all.'

'Really?'

'When I told him that we could settle everything through his solicitor, he said that he wanted to come across. Which is a shame, because if anything, I was hoping for a visit over there. He wants to see where he's from and all that.'

'I suppose he does. I'd be curious too, I guess. Will he meet George?'

'Oh, Gramps will insist. He'll probably pay his fare over here just to make sure of it! More importantly, he wants to meet *you*.'

'Me?'

'Absolutely. He wants to thank you personally for everything. Without you, none of this would've happened.'

'Maybe, let's see.' I couldn't go back on my word to Sarah.

'*Let's see?* Are you joking? Of course you must meet him. You can hardly say no to the poor man. I'll give you a call when I know what's happening.'

I put down the phone and crumpled. *How could I credibly say no to meeting Ned? And Anna would be so pleased. But then I'd need her to lie to Sarah – how would that work?* It was hopeless. At some point it would get out and Sarah would never speak to me again.

As hard-nosed as it seemed, I needed to say no, and vowed to tell James in our next conversation.

TWENTY-SIX

Ned arrived on a Friday that shone full of promise. James had piled on the pressure, making it impossible for me to duck out. I hadn't mentioned anything to Anna. I wanted to play my final part and let the day pass as unremarkably as possible.

George Locke splashed out for Ned to stay at the Crown Hotel, just off the Strand and not far from his Lincoln's Inn Fields' offices. James arranged for a car to collect Ned from the airport and for me to meet him at his hotel bar, before we had dinner.

I caught the tube to Holborn and walked down through Drury Lane, weaving in and out of tourists gathering for an evening at the theatre. As the Crown Hotel appeared, excitement prickled in my stomach.

I pushed my way around the stiff, revolving doors and crossed the marbled lobby. I entered the bar scanning for a man on his own and found several. A balding man, dressed in grey trousers and a yellow pullover, peered and caught my eye.

'Hi, is it Peter?'

I approached. 'Ned?' I'd visualised him younger, thinner and handsome, but he was chubby with a bulbous nose and puffy eyes set too close together. He looked ragged from his long journey.

'Why, yes, it is. Hello!' He thrust forward his hand and shook mine for many seconds. 'You're the guy that's made all this possible.'

'Yes, you could say that.' I claimed back my thoroughly shaken hand.

'It's so great to meet you! Let me buy you a drink.'

'I'll have a Coke, please.' I wanted a clear mind.

'Coke? Are you sure? Barman, a Coke for my friend, please, and... I'll have another neat one. I shouldn't, really, I've already had two. But you know, it's been a hell of a journey, and that drive from the airport, shish! The traffic made Boston look like a breeze, and that's saying something. Line after line after line. That's what I heard, in England they like to line up.'

The barman set out our drinks.

'Thanks, and keep the change.' Ned handed over a note; I didn't catch the colour, but the barman looked delighted.

'Peter, let me tell you about the time I stayed in Chicago.' Ned rattled on about a work trip where he had to queue for breakfast every morning and then launched straight into a story about his car breaking down at the airport. Work had already fried my brain and I wasn't sure how long I could concentrate on his monologue. Ned's airport story moved on to fishing. I stared at him, wondering how different he'd be if Edward had raised him. I imagined him with an Edinburgh brogue... no, it really didn't fit.

When I tuned back in, he was talking about his house, his wife Barbara, his two sons Bobby and Matt, and his job as a high-school science teacher. Finding no opportunity to join in, I decided we'd talk about Edward over dinner. Then Ned yawned.

'You know, Peter, I think the plan is that we eat tonight. I'm absolutely beat, though. I think I'll have something in my room.' The man had no shame. 'Let's put this off until tomorrow. We're meeting up right?'

That wasn't my plan. 'I think I'm working. Perhaps we could talk about Ed—'

'Geez, what I really need is a hot shower, another whisky and then bed. Tell you what, let's meet here tomorrow at noon. What d'ya say? And then you can tell me all about my old dad and his crazy search for me.'

'I might be able—'

'Good man!' He slapped me on the back. 'I knew you'd understand.' Then he drained his glass, wiped his mouth with the back of his hand and walked off towards the lobby, calling, 'See you tomorrow.'

I sat on the tube, seething, not believing what had happened. All that effort just to end up forced into another meeting, another opportunity to sit through Ned's endless drone. And if I wasn't careful, he'd be having such a great time, he'd want to book me for Sunday too. I imagined us bumping into Anna… and then I remembered… Anna! We were supposed to be spending Saturday at the Tate. Anxious to get hold of her, I called from outside the tube station. I told her something had come up and that I needed to work, the involuntary lie irritating me. We put off the Tate until Sunday and arranged for her to stay at mine Saturday night.

I walked home amongst the Friday-night revellers, the usual types milling around the main street, dropping into pubs on their way to other places. As I turned into the backstreets, I felt someone behind me – the same thing that had happened a few weeks before.

I walked a little further and sensed someone at my back. I pushed on, but my neck tickled – a whisper of air, a breath

161

on my skin. I turned again. Shadows skulked in doorways, but no one appeared.

I spun and practically ran. When I finally reached home, I checked one last time.

Across the street, a woman stood – a spectral figure in a long, black coat, with a face that was hidden in shadow. She seemed to be waiting for someone; perhaps she was waiting for me? The thought wasn't a pleasing one, so I hurried into my block and made sure I'd locked the door.

Inside my flat, I went to the lounge window, creeping closer to look out without being seen from outside.

The woman had gone.

And then I had a terrifying, crazy thought.

Could she be standing behind me? My heart stopped for a beat and my legs tingled. I said a silent prayer to any deity who could hear me and slowly turned to look.

Of course, she wasn't there.

'Get a grip, Peter.' I shook my head and grabbed the whisky. As I did, an overpowering scent of roses hit me. 'What the hell is that?' I scanned the flat, looking for the source. I sniffed my clothes and then my fingers but couldn't find the smell. Giving up, I curled off the top of the bottle, poured out the last dregs and knocked them back. The fierce liquid barely touched the sides and I cursed myself for forgetting to buy more. I went to the kitchen to search the cupboards, but I'd drunk the place dry. Unless I wanted to go back outside, to face whatever was out there, the night would be a sober one with nothing to dull my nerves. Feeling exhausted anyway, I called it an early night.

I lay comfortably, with the full moon pouring into the room, rousing me with its brightness. I half remembered drawing the curtains, but they were open. Rolling on my side, away from the shine, I drifted back into sleep. A touch, like a breath, tickled my cheek, but through a squint I saw nothing and floated away again. But then something touched my shoulder and my eyes flicked open.

There, stood a woman with piercing blue eyes. I sprang from her pale, dreadful face and flew out of bed, stretching and grasping for the door. I ripped it open, slammed it behind me and ran naked to the lobby. Trembling, I wrestled my coat from the stand and wrapped it over my body.

My heart pounded in the silence as I weighed up my next move. I had to go back out and face it; I couldn't hide all night.

I swallowed and steeled my nerves, clenching my fists to feel stronger. I crept back to the lounge, then towards the bedroom. My shaking hand grasped the handle and, wincing, I pushed open the door.

She was gone. I scanned the room and confirmed no trace of her. But I couldn't stay in that room. I pulled the door tight, crossed the lounge and dropped into my chair. The image of those eyes burned into my mind. I remembered George's description and knew it must be Katherine. She had a terrible idea of encouragement.

I looked to the whisky for sedation, but the cold, clear glass was as empty as my hopes. I faced a grim voyage to the morning.

TWENTY-SEVEN

I woke, squashed awkward against the chair arm. My legs were numb and my back stiff. I stretched out and cramp tore through my calf, forcing me to jump up and stamp it out. I felt tight, my shoulders solid with tension.

I was being haunted again.

And that's why I had to finish it that day. Finish it with Ned, who should have heard me out already. This time, I needed to stand my ground, complete my part and then put it all behind me.

To change my mood, I took a bath. The steaming depth welcomed and caressed my shattered body, and a mountain of stress drained away. I washed my hair and lingered over a wet shave, and by the time the foam melted, I was a different man.

At ten-to-twelve, I marched through the hotel doors, into a lobby bustling with people. I weaved through the throng and found my way to the bar. The barman took my order of a coffee and offered to bring it over, so I chose a comfy-looking wingback chair.

I sipped at the rich, nutty coffee and watched the swarm of people. Time crept to twenty-past and there was no sign of Ned. Several hotel officials stood in serious conversation, then two uniformed policemen walked out of the lift and joined the discussion. Wondering what was happening, I knocked back my dregs and decided to act.

As I approached reception, one of the suited brigade ushered me towards the concierge at the side of the lobby. I competed with several others in a disorderly queue and, at my first chance, snatched my turn. The concierge cocked his ear to hear over the hubbub.

'I'm here to meet a friend. Can you call his room and tell him I'm here, please? I can't remember his room number, but his name is Ned Clayton.'

The concierge's head snapped up. 'Please wait here a moment, sir.' He rose and paced over to one of the men in suits. They talked back and forth and then the suited man walked over.

'Hello, Mr…?'

'Tyler.'

'Mr Tyler, I'm Mr Davis, the hotel manager. Please take a seat in the lobby and someone will be over to speak with you.' His eyes avoided being drawn into conversation as he directed me towards two red sofas.

'Well… okay.'

I sat facing reception and waited, weighing up the commotion from a new perspective. After a few minutes, a less formal-looking man sat down opposite. He was clean-shaven with short, greying hair. A sureness hung about him that I instantly disliked.

'Good afternoon, Mr Tyler, my name is Detective Sergeant Palmer. How are you?'

'I'm good, thanks. A little confused.'

'Yes, I can imagine. Can I ask how you know Mr Clayton?'

Not prepared for qualifying my relationship with Ned to the police, I felt myself flush. 'I'm a friend of the family and I'm looking after him during his visit. He came over from America yesterday and we were due to meet at twelve today in the hotel bar. We're having lunch.' I became conscious of over-explaining.

'Aha, I see. And when was the last time you saw Mr Clayton?' DS Palmer opened his notebook and started writing, disconcerting me even more.

'Could you tell me why you're asking?'

'I'll come to that in a minute, sir, I just need a few details first. The last time you saw him?'

'I met him here yesterday evening, and we parted around eight-thirty.'

He continued to make notes. 'And then what did you do?'

'I went home.' DS Palmer looked up. 'I took the tube home. I've come back today to meet him for lunch.'

'And why is Mr Clayton in England?'

'He's here on family business. Look, Detective… Palmer, I'm happy to answer your questions, but can you at least tell me what's going on? Please?'

DS Palmer stared, weighing me up, and then leant forward in an attempt at intimacy. 'I'm sorry to tell you this, but Mr Clayton was found dead this morning.'

'*Dead?*' Heads in the lobby turned.

'Yes, I'm afraid so.' I sat silent, struggling to understand, and after letting it sink in for a moment, he added, 'I know it's difficult, and I'm sorry, but I'm trying to piece everything together. If you could give me a few more minutes of your time, I'd really appreciate it.'

'Of course.' I sank back.

'What sort of business was he here for?' He was ready

again with his pen. I explained about the inheritance and gave him George Locke's details.

'And do know his next of kin?'

'That'll be his wife, Barbara, in Boston. Mr Locke should have her details.'

'Don't worry, we'll sort that out.' DS Palmer made more notes.

'If it helps, he might have been unwell yesterday evening.'

'Unwell?'

'Yes. We were supposed to have dinner and he called it off at the last minute. He didn't feel up to it.'

'Did he say why?'

'Just said he was tired. He'd had a long journey.'

'Nothing else?'

'No.'

DS Palmer fixed me with another evaluating look. 'Sorry to break this to you, but it looks like Mr Clayton committed suicide.'

'*Suicide?* But that's not possible. Why would he do that?'

'Yes, I know. It's always a shock. Especially when you've just seen him.'

'But… are you *sure?*'

'I can't say too much, Mr Tyler. You understand. But it seems he jumped from his window. At this stage, we're not treating his death as suspicious. But if there's anything odd you remember, it could be a big help.'

'It doesn't make sense. He'd travelled all this way to be here. He was about to receive a fortune.'

'I'm sorry. Suicides often make no sense.'

'Did he leave a note or anything? Surely he would've left a note if it was suicide.'

'I can't give out too many details…' Then he'd thought of

something. 'Actually, this was on his bedside table.' He fished into his inside coat pocket and produced a photograph. 'I believe it's his mother. I wondered if it had some relevance.'

I saw a woman, possibly in her early thirties, sitting on a picnic bench. She was holding a glass of wine and smiling for the camera. I turned over the photo and written on the back was 'Mom, White Mountains, June 1933'. I didn't recognise her at all, and my mind switched to the previous night's haunting. If this was Katherine, who the hell was in my room?

'Are you alright?'

'Yes.' I zoned back in. 'His mother died some years ago, in America. He probably brought the photo because of the trip.' He looked at me blankly. 'He wanted to see where he came from. His mother was from England too.'

'A bit like a family reunion.'

His words struck a terrible chord.

He took the photo and tucked it back into his pocket. 'I think that's all I need for now. Can I take your contact details in case there's something later?'

I gave him my home address and work number.

'And here's my card, if there's anything else you think of.'

When we stood up to say goodbye, my head swam.

'You sure you're alright?'

'Yes, thanks, just... I wasn't expecting...'

'Perhaps you should stay here a bit.'

'No, really. I'll be fine.'

And with that I stumbled to the doors, out into the fresh afternoon. I drank down deep draughts of air, trying to quell the shock and gain some equilibrium, and found myself walking back aimlessly through Drury Lane. I needed a stiff drink and thankfully the nearest pub was in sight, but I also needed someone to talk to. I felt in my pocket for change and crossed the street to the phone box.

TWENTY-EIGHT

The smoky pub buzzed with lunchtime drinkers, and it took a fair few waves of a ten-pound note to catch the barman's attention. Taking the opportunity, I ordered two large whiskies. I downed one and carried the other to the only free table.

While I waited, I brooded on Ned and my last conversation with Anna – she didn't even know he'd been found. She'd kept her side of the bargain and let the whole thing go, because I'd asked her to, for Michael's sake. This was going to be tricky. I wished my head felt clearer.

She rushed in and spotted me through the crowd.

'Hi.' She bent and kissed me on the lips.

'What can I get you?' I stood.

'I'll have a dry white wine, please.'

The bar rush had died down and I soon returned with the wine and another whisky.

'What's happened? What's the emergency?'

'It's Ned. Anna, he's dead.'

'Oh no! That's awful… and so frustrating. When did it happen?'

'Last night.'

169

'*Last night?*'

'Or the early hours of this morning, probably.'

'What... how do you know?'

'The police have just told me.'

'Hang on, I'm lost. Rewind a bit. Why would the police contact you?'

'Ned came over from America yesterday and—'

'How do you know?'

'James got in touch. They found him and he wanted to meet me.'

'When?'

'Today.'

'James got in touch today?'

'No, a few weeks ago.' I was losing this. 'I came to meet Ned today.'

'*You* spoke to James a few weeks ago and arranged to see Ned?'

'Not exactly that. I didn't say yes.' She stared at me in strong silence, and I shifted and looked away. 'I didn't want any fuss. I didn't actually want to meet him, but James made it impossible to say no.'

'You've been doing all this, and you've not shared one word with me?'

'I wanted to, but—'

'You even rang yesterday, to put me off. And like an idiot, I believed you.'

'No, it wasn't like—'

'And Michael... We agreed for *Michael's* sake. You made me feel like a monster when I wanted to be part of this. What does that make *you?*'

'I should've talked to you. Sorry, I admit it. I've messed up.'

'I can't believe your nerve.'

'Look, I'm sorry. Very sorry. But I need to talk to you. The police are saying—'

'I don't care! I'm not interested.' She gathered her bag and stood. 'You've managed by yourself so far, so carry on. I've already rearranged my life around you this weekend, and I don't know why I bothered. Will I ever be able to trust you?'

'Anna—'

'No, Peter. I can assure you, it won't help if I stay.'

She swung her bag over her shoulder, turned and walked out.

Out of the corner of my eye, I saw the people on the next table staring. I glared at them, and they looked away, but a knowing smirk passed between them, and I wanted to throw their drinks in their faces.

Damn! Damn! Damn! my head screamed. Everything I touched turned to shit. I knocked back my whisky and stared at the empty glass. It was early afternoon, and I could fit in a few dozen more. *After all, I should avoid going home to see Edward.*

I remembered the photo of Katherine that DS Palmer had shown me and how she didn't look like the woman in my room. And then I had a thought: *What if it was Faye? What if she was warning me off from helping her cheating husband?* With my finger on the inside of the rim, I twirled the empty glass in circles, thinking. Then Mr Locke's words came to me: *'Faye's portrait is hanging in the theatre where her father was patron.'*

I went back to the bar.

'Do you have a Yellow Pages?' I called over to the barman.

He collected it from near the till. 'Anything else?'

'Another whisky,' my tongue tried to say, but I trapped it. I stood fighting, dying for another taste of that fiery burst and desperate to escape how bad I was feeling. But knowing that I needed a clear, sharp mind, a bit of grit kicked in. 'I'll have a Coke.'

Back at the table I thumbed to the long list of theatres. Almost all of them sounded familiar, but the moment I got to 'S', I knew it. *That's it!* I thumped the pages. *The Shrewsbury, Russell Street. That's literally around the corner.*

I gulped down my Coke, picked up my coat and left.

Within minutes, I found myself standing in front of the Shrewsbury Theatre. The posters outside advertised *The Importance of Being Earnest,* and given the time, I knew a matinee performance would be in full flow. I walked through the double glass swing doors into a world of gaudy glitz, clashing red and purple walls and a smell of old ticket stubs. Out of synch with the performance, it felt forbidden to be there, so I crept quietly and respectfully to the ticket counter, where two women sat chatting. They broke off at the unexpected intrusion.

'Can I help you?' the younger woman said.

'Actually, I'm here on an unusual errand.' The women stared. 'I believe there's a painting of a relative hanging here and I'd like to take a look at it. Is that possible?'

'We have loads of paintings here, darling, what's it look like?'

'Well, I don't know exactly. It'll be a painting of a lady… in her twenties… or thirties, I think.' They rightly looked blank. 'Her father was patron of the theatre and—'

The older woman cut in. 'Oh, that'll be the big one, Sue, on the stairs to the circle.' Sue nodded in agreement.

'Great, you know it. Do you mind if I take a quick look?'

'Nah, we don't mind anything much,' said Sue. 'Feel free, the stairs are over there.'

I made my way to the shallow stairs and paused to take in the moment. I set off, glancing around the walls at the procession of actors from musicals gone by. When the staircase turned back on itself, a portrait in an ornate gold frame faced me. In a trance of fascination, I drew closer, my heart racing and a sweat breaking down my back. The woman looked the right age and of the right era, but if this was Faye, it wasn't her who had terrified me. I checked the frame, but there was no nameplate and the artist's signature, 'Thomas Gilbert', gave nothing away.

Not wanting to make assumptions, I climbed up to the first-floor lobby to check the paintings there. I found three, but none were portraits.

Accepting that I'd found Faye, I returned to have a closer look. Her eyes smiled down, radiating serenity, and I could see why Edward had fallen for her all those years before. Her face beamed with a spirit of youth and hope, and for the first time, I felt true sadness for her. I looked her in the eye and gave a nod of respect.

Not sure where I stood in terms of my research, I rested against the banister and suddenly felt drained. My legs almost buckled as stress and lack of sleep caught up, and I realised that standing on stairs wasn't the best idea. Looking around, I saw a sign to the bar and made my way up for a drink.

With the performance still showing, the bar was empty except for a slim, middle-aged bartender who stood with his back to me, replenishing the shelves with clean glasses. He was holding a wine glass up to the light when he sensed me and turned.

'Hello, can I help you?' He was surprised to have a customer.

'Any chance of a glass of water?'

'Of course.' He selected a pint glass and turned to the sink to fill it. 'Here you go.'

I took it and drank half straight off. 'Lovely, thank you. I needed that.'

'I can tell. Decided to give the performance a miss then?'

'No, actually, I've just popped in to look at a painting.'

'Oh really, which one?'

'The one of Faye Featherstone.' I drank another draught. 'Her father was patron of the theatre.'

'Ah, that one there then.'

Looking up, I saw him nodding past my shoulder. I turned and froze. The same piercing, blue eyes stared down from a china-white face, striking ice into my soul.

About to pass out, I stumbled to the nearest chair. The barman's words cut through.

'Sir, *sir!* Are you okay?' He shook me to my senses.

'No, sorry…'

'Stay here, I'll get Betty.' He dashed out of the room and returned moments later with the older ticket woman.

'Goodness, Ted, he looks shocking!'

'He's had a funny turn, I think.'

'Look after him, I'll fetch some tea.'

I heard the lobby fill up with people leaving the performance, the hubbub of voices sounding far off in a dreamland. Despite being out of it, I knew I'd embarrassed myself and stood to escape.

'You're not going anywhere until you've drunk every drop of this tea, young man.' Eagle-eyed Betty wasn't to be fooled, and I slumped back down. She passed me a cup and saucer of strong orange tea.

'Thank you.' I took it and drank. It tasted disgustingly sweet, but after a few mouthfuls, I managed to drain the cup. 'I feel much better.'

'You should stay here a while.' Betty took the cup from my hands.

'I'm fine. I need to get going.'

'Already? Well, at least let me find you a cab. You shouldn't go off on your own.' She nodded to Ted, who left without waiting for my consent. 'Are you well enough to leave? I don't want you going off too quick.'

'Honestly, I'll be fine. I'm just tired. I'll feel better in the fresh air.'

'Well, if you're sure. Come on, I'll help you down.'

Ignoring the painting, I stood and gained my balance. Still worried for me, Betty grabbed my arm and linked it as we walked. We met Ted outside, where he helped me into the waiting cab. I flopped onto the back seat and Ted closed the door.

'Where you going, mate?' The taxi driver adjusted his rear-view mirror to see me.

I couldn't face the thought of going home and nor was I fit for company.

'Actually, I want to stay in a hotel tonight.'

'Blimey, whereabouts, mate?' He just wanted to start the meter.

'Somewhere nearby… Charring Cross, maybe? I just can't think where at the moment.'

'What?! Are you sure?'

'Can we just drive there for now?'

He stared, looking disgusted, grumbling about the time it was taking to earn a tiny fare. Within five minutes, we were driving along the backstreets around the station. I spotted the Olympia Hotel.

'Here will do fine, thanks.' To make it up to him, I let him keep the change from a tenner and he welcomed it with a, 'Have a very good evening, mate.' He probably thought I'd be spending it with a prostitute.

At the cupboard that masqueraded as a reception, I asked

175

the girl for a single room. I paid up front and she handed me a weighty, round metal fob with one key dangling from it. There was no lift, so I climbed the narrow stairs to the second floor and negotiated the dim tunnel of rooms to number twenty-four.

The stale den boasted outdated, cup-marked furniture, ill-fitting red velvet curtains and a stained pink carpet. On the single bed, two sagging white pillows lay stacked on top of one another, advertising their lack of support, and the white duvet cover looked grey. But it would do. I threw my jacket onto the white plastic chair, kicked off my shoes and crashed out on the bed.

I woke confused and saw my father scowling down at me. Then it wasn't my father; it was the image of Edward I'd created in my mind. My eyes widened with alarm, but then I realised, it was a shadow cast by the streetlight's eerie glow.

I checked my watch – it was five-to-one – and forced myself up. In a drugged haze, I stumbled to the bathroom for a pee and slurped a drink from the limescale-furred tap. With the distractions of the day, I'd not eaten since breakfast and my stomach cramped. The tea tray was my only hope, and my luck was in for a change, when I found two mini-packs of bourbon biscuits. I clicked on the kettle and, while it boiled, munched through all six biscuits. As I poured the boiled water over a tea bag, moisture wafted over my face, bringing a metallic scent. I added a sugar for energy and then tipped in a cap-full of milk. But before the beige liquid hit my lips, I burst into fits of tears. Overcome with exhaustion and sorrow, I sobbed and sobbed.

Whatever had happened to Ned, I now knew Faye's spite was at the heart of it, and all my actions had aided her terrible revenge. If I wanted peace of mind, there'd be none from Edward. And none from the shame that I was truly 'Peter Tyler, Total Fuck-Up of the World'. Curling up on the bed, I wept with the weight of my wasted efforts and cried myself back to sleep.

TWENTY-NINE

After Ned's death, I had no intention of staying in my flat and asked David if I could use his spare room. I told him that my landlord needed to fix a water leak, and without questioning, David took me in. He saw it as a good excuse for premarital drinking and was unimpressed when I said that I was off the stuff. '*Letting the side down again, old boy!*'

On the Monday following Ned's death, I called James and found that the police had already spoken to him.

'Bloody awful business,' James said.

'Still can't believe it, really.'

'So how did he come across? Was he acting off his trolley?'

'No, not at all. Quite the opposite.'

'If it helps, the police have spoken to his wife, and apparently he had a history of depression.'

'Did he? He seemed so... positive about everything. It doesn't make sense. Why bother travelling all the way over here?'

'Perhaps he wanted to come full circle – back to where he belonged and all that. Who knows?' James was suitably detached.

'What happens now?' I asked.

'I'll contact his widow and arrange the transfer of Edward's estate to her. Though that can't be done until after the inquest.'

'Inquest?'

'Certainly. And I expect you'll be called to give evidence.' This was never going to end.

'I suppose so. Well, thanks for your help. I'm sorry it didn't turn out better for George. How is he, by the way?'

'Devastated, to be honest. He doesn't want to talk about it. He wants me to finish it and doesn't want to be involved.'

'Oh, that's sad. Totally understandable, though. Please send him my regards.'

I put down the phone, thinking of my meeting with George. It was only three months later but felt more like three years. He'd come so close to putting things right for his friend. Poor old George.

THIRTY

I felt depressed, swamped by a deep numbness that wouldn't shift. Sarah called a couple of times, more out of duty than interest. We found little to say and her forced efforts only made me feel worse.

I tried to make it up to Anna. By way of apology, I bought theatre tickets and called round with flowers. At first, things felt fine, but I'd sunk so low that I couldn't keep my efforts up. My shower of attention turned into a dribble, and we spoke less and less. How could I expect Anna to take pleasure in my company, when I couldn't even stand myself? After several lacklustre dating disasters, we never met up again.

In the office I clung on. I survived. Philip couldn't complain because he got his pound of flesh – working around the clock came easy, a welcome pursuit. However, Philip still kept his distance. I didn't care. I ran and ran on my hamster wheel, wondering at the point of it all.

As my 'temporary' stay at David's ticked into months, he lost patience with his miserable little brother crowding his space. He couldn't understand what was taking so long and put pressure on me to move back home. I told him that I'd fallen out with the landlord and started looking for somewhere else. When David realised I was serious, he suggested that I saved my fees and bought his place. The timing was perfect, so I agreed and that got him off my case. My own flat became the most expensive storage in London, but I just couldn't motivate myself to clear it. I decided to wait until after the wedding, when I could shift everything in one go.

With living arrangements settled, David relaxed again, giving me breathing space. Our focus switched to his impending wedding, and I looked forward to healing things with Sarah face to face. But then a letter came that knocked me back to square one – it was the summons to attend Ned's inquest.

It was a blazing August day, and I could think of a million better things to do than go to the coroner's court. At least it was a chance to meet James in the flesh. He was plumper than I'd imagined, with receding, mousey hair and oversized, sticking-out ears. Despite the years between them, I could see George's likeness in his round face.

'We meet at last,' he said as he shook my hand.

'Indeed. It's good to put a name to the face.'

'We're in for an interesting day, no doubt.' We turned to walk into the court.

'Just as long as Ned can rest in peace, it'll be worth it.' They sounded like noble words. In truth, it was I who wanted the peace.

We filtered along the aisle and sat down on purple-upholstered bench seats. This court felt too new and clinical, lacking any presence of history and tradition. Three feet high, wooden partitions demarked where they'd pen in a jury and where the witness should sit. The coroner's seat was slightly raised, but instead of a grand, high-backed throne, it was just an ordinary chair. The walls were plain, standard-issue cream.

At this hearing there was no jury, just the coroner in a suit. He looked around sixty with thin, combed-back grey hair and carried an inoffensive amount of authority. He sat, introduced himself and explained the order of the day's proceedings.

Dr Chandra, the medical expert, was the first witness called. A man in his forties, wearing a black three-piece suit, took the stand. He stated that Ned's body showed signs of trauma consistent with injuries sustained from a fall of seventy feet. He'd suffered vertebral compression fractures and had died from a cerebral haemorrhage. He'd consumed around twelve units of alcohol.

The coroner called DS Palmer next. He was dressed much smarter than on the day we'd met. He flipped open his notebook, cleared his throat with a cough and took the court through his investigations. He said he'd found no signs of foul play and concluded that Mr Clayton had committed suicide. He said that the court would hear evidence of Mr Clayton's circumstances and state of mind to support his conclusion. He proposed that, by dying on English soil and subject to English law, Mr Clayton believed that the claim to his inheritance would be more straightforward for his family.

Then I was called. I didn't feel nervous at first, but as I walked to the stand with all eyes on me, my legs turned to jelly. In a dry voice, I recounted the events of the evening before Ned's death. I confirmed that he seemed in good spirits and gave no indication that he was upset and suicidal. The coroner nodded and let me go.

The next witness was Stephen Harris, a young man from the room service staff. I watched him fidget and pick at his fingers and felt glad that it wasn't just me who was handling it clumsily. He gave an account of taking Ned two double whiskies just before midnight.

'So, he ordered two drinks? Was someone else with him?' the coroner asked.

'Not that I saw. I think both drinks were for him.'

'And did you notice anything out of the ordinary about Mr Clayton?'

'Well… not at the time. I mean, knowing what he did after, it does sound odd now.'

'Go on.'

'He asked me if the hotel was haunted.' Muted laughter rippled through the court, though not mine. Mr Harris looked wounded. 'I wouldn't have mentioned it, but he did look… shook-up, I suppose.'

James leaned over. 'I think he'd had enough whisky already.'

'Please tell us about the conversation,' the coroner continued.

'He asked me whether the hotel was haunted, and I said that years ago, a maid had fallen down the lift shaft and some people had reckoned to have seen her ghost. He said he was sorry to hear that and then he tipped me a fiver and I left.'

'And how would you describe his general mood?'

'I suppose, looking back, he seemed in a bad mood.'

'A bad mood? What do you mean by that?'

'Not quite angry. Annoyed, maybe… and a bit on edge. It looked like he'd been in bed – the covers were all messed up and that – and he was in his pyjamas. So, I thought he'd been woken up and perhaps couldn't get back to sleep. And that's why I thought he was in a bad mood.'

The coroner thanked Mr Harris and let him go, not seeing any relevance in Ned's disturbed sleep. I bit my tongue, caught between the madness of calling out that we needed to know more and keeping intact my reputation as a sane human being.

The next witness was Elizabeth Wainwright, a solicitor acting for Ned's wife. She read out a statement on her client's behalf. It revealed that Ned was battling with a drink problem and suffering from extreme mood swings. Coupled with this, he'd been having an affair that had ended only a few days prior to his England trip.

On the balance of it all, there was no surprise when the coroner ruled Ned's death as suicide.

Outside court, James shook my hand. 'That's the end of it then. Sad old business.'

'Yes. A hard end to a long search.'

'Well, on behalf of Gramps, thank you for all that you did.'

'We tried our best – it just wasn't to be, I suppose.'

'No. But at least we got to meet each other. Perhaps we could go for a drink sometime.' It was an easier way to say goodbye, and with the idea offered, we parted.

Reflecting on the hearing, I still struggled to accept that the man I'd met at the hotel that evening was suicidal, regardless of his personal baggage. Then DS Palmer's words about suicides often making no sense floated back. But many things still troubled me – Ned jumping from a window and his affair break-up, just like Edward. And then Ned asking about hotel hauntings. And more to the point, I'd seen Faye's ghost maybe at the exact time that Ned had jumped. Did that mean Faye was to blame in some way for Ned's death? Was that so ridiculous?

THIRTY-ONE

After months of build-up, September the 3rd arrived on a breeze strong enough to bend the sturdiest leafy Chelsea trees. The sun hid in the clouds – a rough day for a white wedding. Despite David's superhero powers, he couldn't sway the gods of the weather.

Hungover, David and I dressed and met up with Nick, his best man and friend since primary school, for a swift pint before arriving at St Mary's. People were already packed into both aisles and I recognised Uncle Terry, Aunt Jane and my cousin, Heather. I nodded at them as David dumped me at the door and took Nick to meet Emma's parents. Used to it, I spotted Sarah at the front and made my way to sit with her. She smiled a thin welcome that didn't reach her eyes and turned to wave at David. I greeted Adam and the boys and sat next to Michael, giving him a wink of encouragement as I ruffled his hair.

'How are you, young man?'

'I'm all dressed up in my best.' I laughed at his echo of Sarah.

'I can see that. Nice shoes.'

'They used to be Andrew's. They don't fit him anymore.'

'Michael, come here and sit with me.' Sarah was patting a space between herself and Adam.

'She'll need to make sure he behaves.' Adam felt the need to explain.

Then the organ leapt into life, and everyone shushed to attention. David waited alongside Nick, looking rather pale. We all stood to watch Lucy walk down the aisle with a cloud of lemon bridesmaids. I watched David's face; I'd never seen him so humble, a mixture of pride, love and terror. Given how much he'd drank in the past twenty-four hours, he was doing remarkably well.

After the service, David and Lucy set off in a vintage Rolls, and we travelled behind in minibuses to the Grosvenor in Mayfair. There we waited for photos, toasted on champagne and ate the wedding breakfast, before resting and returning for the evening do. Not knowing anyone else, I stuck to Sarah and Adam, but Sarah was on hot bricks and hard to engage. She spent the evening dipping in and out of conversations with Lucy's family, leaving me with Adam.

Adam shouted over Abba, 'Ignore her, she'll get over it. She's just overprotective.'

So, it wasn't my imagination; she was avoiding me.

'How is Michael?' I asked.

'He's okay. He still has nightmares and imaginary friends. Who didn't at his age?'

Here was my chance. 'Yes, I had an imaginary friend as a boy. David and Sarah made my life a misery as usual. His name was John. I always wanted to be called John, after John in *Swallows and Amazons*.'

'What, instead of Peter from *The Lion, Witch and the Wardrobe*?'

'Hey, yes. Well remembered.'

'It was my sister's favourite. She was always reading it.'

'No, it was always John for me.' I manoeuvred the conversation back.

'Well, Michael's friend is a lady.'

'A *lady*?' My blood ran cold. 'Not even a girl?' My curiosity flipped into obsession.

'I know, it is a bit odd, I suppose.'

'Do you know any more about her?'

'What, apart from she doesn't really exist?' He eyed me like I was daft. 'Sarah won't let him talk about it.'

Michael and Andrew ran over and grabbed their drinks, glugging them as if they were about to die of thirst.

'Hiya, fellas, what you been up to?' Adam pulled Andrew closer.

'Playing tag with Fraser, Melanie and Simon,' Andrew said between gulps, 'and the others.'

'Have you seen Mum?'

'Nu-uh,' Michael said.

'I need the toilet.' Andrew ran off.

'I'm going to the bar, want another?' Adam asked me.

'Yes, please.'

Adam got up and I found myself alone with Michael. I watched him finishing his lemonade and knew I shouldn't risk upsetting his evening. I just couldn't help myself.

'Are you having a good time?'

'Yep.'

'I still have that picture you drew for me.' He looked up, trying to think. 'Of me reading you a story.'

'Yes! I remember. When will you come again?'

'I'm not sure. Would you like me to come?'

'Yes, but I don't want those dreams.'

'What dreams?'

He looked at me, doubting he should answer.

187

'What are they about?'

'About my friend looking for you and Edward.'

Edward?! '…Who's your friend?'

'Mummy says I can't talk about it. I'm not allowed.'

'Can't you even tell me her name?'

'Whose name?' I jumped at Sarah's voice.

'My friend's name,' Michael said before I could stop him. 'I didn't talk about it, I promise. Uncle Peter asked me.'

She turned on me. 'What exactly did you ask him?'

'I didn't mean any harm – I was just trying to let Michael know that it's okay, that we've all been there.'

'Why on earth would you do that when you know how I feel?'

'I was trying to help, that's all.'

'By ignoring me?'

'I just thought he might want to talk about it.'

'What on earth gives you the right to stir all this up?' I saw Sarah's anger rise as a red line on her chest.

'I don't mean any—'

'You have no idea what we've been through. *No idea!*' Heads turned.

Adam came over and put down the two pints. 'It's okay—'

'*No, it isn't!* Why did you leave him with Michael?'

'Sarah, it's Peter.'

'You *know* what I'm talking about.' She put her palms to her cheeks in exasperation and shook her head. 'Adam, I think it's time to go.'

'Come on, Sarah,' I tried. 'Don't go, it's David's wedding, for heaven's sake.'

'Yes, thank you, I realise that.' She turned to Adam. 'Michael should be going to bed.'

'Okay.' Adam knew when to give up. 'I'll find Andrew.'

'Sarah—'

'You need to keep away from Michael. If I can't trust you to be alone with him even for five minutes, you just need to stay away.' She snatched her bag and left Adam to usher the boys. I watched her kiss David and Lucy goodbye; they were too drunk to notice or care.

I drank down my lager and then sipped at Adam's sour beer. I stared from chair to chair, the empty places mirroring just how I felt. Why on earth had I pushed it when it was far too late to help Ned? This nonsense had to stop. I thumped the table in frustration and swore to sort myself out.

THIRTY-TWO

The weekend after the wedding, I moved the last of David's things to his new house, while he honeymooned. Then I needed to clear my own flat, the thing I'd dreaded the most. I'd only popped back twice since Ned's death, rushing in to grab things as if the place had been on fire.

When I walked around the rooms, everything seemed normal, not a hint of the menace that had stalked me before. But I was far from having fond memories of the place and had moved on a mile from it feeling like home. The September light showed up the flat's scruffiness and I wondered how I'd stood it for so long.

I started emptying drawers in the bedroom, stuffing what was left into bin sacks, and before long was working at pace. I methodically swept through the bedroom, bathroom and kitchen, and deliberately left the lounge until last. As I crept into enemy territory, the sideboard stood grinning – a sinister face of doors and drawers. I walked over and curled my fingers around its handle. I could still feel the book's essence, spreading up my arm and into my nerves. I held my breath and opened it.

I stared into a dark hole – a mouth, waiting. Bracing myself for the bite, I reached in. My fingers found the contents and I scooped them out, watching as they fell onto the floor. And there, at my feet, the dreadful thing lay. I picked it up. Now, without struggling, I could read the scrawl: *'Find me in death – bye, bye.'* The words turned cold on my tongue and fuelled my desire to get out. But before I could move my feet, I felt it. Something rising behind me, growing and gaining in strength.

A low, wheezing breath moaned a whisper of my name. My heart stopped and I listened. Then, like a serpent, closer and closer slid the scraping along the floor.

I almost passed out, but primal survival focused my nerves. I screwed my eyes tight and as the sound scraped through my body, I used all my strength to will it away.

It stopped.

I stood, hardly breathing.

A hand grabbed my ankle. I shrieked and lost balance and tumbled to the floor. I scrambled backwards, kicking, screaming and fighting.

But nothing was there.

I sprang to my feet and rammed those last bits into the bag. In a flash, I snatched the sacks and threw them onto the landing. I picked up the keys, almost losing them in my shakes. Then I yanked the door shut and sealed it for good.

THIRTY-THREE

I woke and heard Elena in the kitchen, making coffee. I closed my eyes and basked in the new-found luxury of a Saturday lie-in.

I'd been going out with Elena for almost a month, a fortunate break in a difficult day. Philip had called a divisional meeting and announced that he'd promoted Ajay. He hadn't involved me in the decision or even had the courtesy to tell me beforehand. It underlined how unimportant I'd become. I was seething but could either join the celebration in the pub or look even more of a loser by bowing out.

Ajay was popular and half the company turned up to celebrate with him. While watching him sparkle, I sulked over my pint, ready to call it a night. Then I noticed Elena alone at the bar and, with a few drinks inside me, swaggered my way over.

'Are you out for the duration?' My snappy chat-up line.

'I'll see how I last.' She leaned in close to be heard above the music. 'How did you get on with Father Ryan by the way?' We hadn't spoken since then.

'He was great. He really helped,' I fibbed.

'He's a good man. We're lucky to have him.'

'Do you want another?'

She looked down at her glass like she'd forgotten she was drinking. 'Yes, please, why not.'

That night, Elena ended up at mine. I was sure that in the morning she'd be mortified about her drunken decisions, but I was wrong – this intelligent, Mediterranean beauty, for some reason, seemed to like me.

I lay with my eyes closed, following the sound of Elena's footsteps into the room. Grinning, I opened my eyes. There was no one there.

'Elena?' I sat up just as she put her head around the door.

'Come and get breakfast. Don't want you fading on me.'

I pulled on a T-shirt and followed her out.

'Did you—'

'Hope you don't mind,' she cut me off, 'I opened some bags to look for coffee filters. Why don't you unpack?'

'Too busy.'

'Too busy waiting for me to do it, more like. Why have you kept this junk?'

'What junk?'

'A stuffed monkey.'

'That's Mr Chimp, my best friend.'

'Mm-huh. A football mug with no handle.'

'Where did you find this stuff?'

'I've barely begun. A prefect's badge. A signed photo of Tommy Cooper—'

'Hey, that's Mum's. Let me see this bag.' I looked in. 'It's stuff from sideboard.' I ignored the hairs rising on my neck and focused on the bag of safe things. 'Look, here's my woggle.'

'Woggle?'

'Scouts wear them. And my first aid certificate. You never know when I might need that.'

She walked over and put her arm around my waist. 'I think I need the kiss of life now. The suspense of what's in there is killing me.' She puckered and we smooched.

'Let's eat breakfast in the bedroom,' I said.

'What a good idea.'

I popped to the loo and found Elena waiting in the covers. The radio was on and Frank Sinatra added a nice touch.

'Looks scrummy,' I said. 'Where's the bacon?'

'Right here.' She leant towards me and kissed my neck with soft travelling pecks. Then she traced her nose up through my chin and planted her mouth on mine. We fell into a long kiss and she groaned into the moment.

'Hey.' I pulled back. 'Listen.'

'What?'

I put up my hand to silence her and she huffed back into the pillows.

'*And your father's book,* The Silent Accusation, *was actually based on a true story?*' the radio declared.

'*That's right. It was a famous tale in its day. My father wanted to bring it to life, excuse the pun. Of course, he exercised a generous amount of poetic licence.*'

'*And your compilation,* The Grim and the Gallows, *includes that original true tale?*'

'*Yes. I've hand-picked twelve cases to illustrate the stories of murder over the last century. I find it fascinating that our appetite for the gruesome remains inherently strong. And that our narratives have matured into quite sophisticated, graphic accounts over the years.*'

'*Interesting stuff. Margaret Abbott, thank you so much for joining us today.*'

'One sec.'

'What?'

'*The Grim and the Gallows* by Margaret Abbot. I need to write that down.'

'Bloody hell.'

I was already scrawling on a magazine lying next to the bed. 'This is unbelievable!'

'Are you going to tell me why it's so marvellous?'

'Well…'

'No? Good. Kiss me!'

'Listen, lady, this is what happens when you do something reckless like turn on the radio.'

'I didn't turn it on, you did.' Before I could protest, her tongue was in my mouth.

THIRTY-FOUR

The next day, I visited Foyles on Charring Cross Road and picked up a copy of Margaret's book. It was a hefty hardback with a misty cemetery on the cover and a headline boasting, 'A century of the most shocking true crimes'. I left it undisturbed in its paper bag until I was home with a whisky. The 'Memoir Murder' was the second story.

As Margaret had hinted, there were differences in the accounts – the true version being even *less* interesting. The man, Jack Collins, was having an affair with his housekeeper, Miss Bradshaw, when he planned the demise of his wife. The police found his left-behind diary, and Mr Collins was arrested and hanged.

Thrilled to find another dull story, I snapped the book shut and tossed it onto the coffee table. I drained my glass and stood to get a top-up just as something moved to my left. When I looked, I'd missed what it was. In an instant, the temperature plummeted to a chill that caught at the back of my throat.

I waited in silence, to see what it meant.

Slowly, in the corner of the room, a shadow crept from the floor and spread across the wall like a seeping, bloody stain. Then came the strange scent of the roses, heady and sweet. But in a moment, their smell turned sour, into a retching stink of decay.

Then something sucked the breath from me, pressing down into my chest, strangling and infecting my heart with agony and despair. I faded and fell to the floor.

THIRTY-FIVE

Sat in the partner's premeet, Philip caught me staring into space twice. I still found it impossible to focus. I was back at square one – a mouse waiting for the eagle to pounce, cowering with the dread of the torture. When the meeting ended, I headed for my office, avoiding the post-meeting chat.

One of the secretaries brought me a coffee and I immediately knocked it over. As I rushed to mop up the mess, the phone rang.

'Hi, Peter, it's James.'

'James, this is a surprise.' *And too much of a coincidence.*

'You're not going to believe this.'

'Try me.'

'Faye is alive.'

'*What?*' I snapped my pen.

'Her solicitor wants the house deeds. I didn't know we had them, but apparently Edward left them in our care.'

'Well… I don't know what to say.' I rubbed my temple. 'She can't be alive—'

'I know. She must be ninety-odd or something. She's definitely still with us, though.'

'Where?'

'In a care home in Kensington. And trying to sell the house so she can pay for it, I suppose.'

I knew that Faye was dead. I'd seen her ghost, for heaven's sake. 'So... what happens now?'

'We hand over the deeds, I guess. And she carries on living in the care home. I knew you'd want to know.'

'Yes... Sorry, which care home?'

'The address I have is Primrose House. Though I probably shouldn't have told you that.'

'I just wondered whether I'd come across it when researching Edward.'

'Don't do anything crazy like track the old girl down and marry her for her money – she'll have none soon.' James laughed. 'Anyway, I'm sure it makes no difference, but I thought I'd share the news.'

'I appreciate it – thanks for letting me know.'

Things were turning crazier. That eagle was on its way.

If I'd expected to concentrate on work, I was a fool. All I could think about was Faye. But with Philip keeping a close eye, I couldn't show signs of weakening. I took a file from my tray and pushed its papers around my desk. Before I could stop them, my fingers dialled Directory Enquiries and then the care home.

'Good morning, Primrose House,' a practised voice sang out.

'Oh, hello. I believe you have a relative of mine living with you, and I'd like to come and see her. Can you tell me your visiting hours, please?'

'Certainly. Anytime between nine in the morning and ten at night. We do prefer to know in advance, if possible. Just to make sure that we're ready for you.'

'So, I could come this evening around seven?'

'Yes, that would be fine. We'll have finished dinner by then. Can I ask who you're visiting?'

'Faye Featherstone.'

'Oh, Faye. That will be a lovely surprise for her.'

'Is it possible to keep it a surprise?' I didn't want the ninety-odd-year-old doing a runner.

'Yes, of course. I don't know how much you know about her health. Even if I told her, she's unlikely to remember five minutes later.'

'Ah.' I wasn't sure whether that was a help or hindrance.

'Righty-o. I'll note you down in the book and we'll expect you around seven, Mr…'

I looked at the name on my file. 'Webster.'

'Mr Webster.'

Elena's annoyance showed as much as her suspicion of my migraine. We were due to meet her friends for drinks and she thought it was my way of avoiding the evening. We left work together and she walked me to the tube, sussing me out. When we reached Bank station, I turned for a kiss.

'Peter!' a voice called.

I turned and stiffened with surprise. 'Anna, how are you?'

Elena sensed my unease and turned towards the threat. Anna carried on oblivious. 'I'm good, thanks. More to the point, *you* look really well. I take it that life's back to normal?'

'Yes, it's all sorted.' I closed down the conversation before Edward was out of the bag. Sensing something amiss, Elena stepped in.

'Hi, I'm Elena. Peter's girlfriend.'

'Sorry, I should've introduced you. Elena, this is Anna. We were at university together.'

'Hi,' Anna said as she looked at Elena and then to me with an expression I couldn't judge. 'Well, I just wanted to say hello.'

'Yes, I'm glad you did. Nice to see you.' I knew that wasn't the reaction she'd wanted, but I needed her gone. With a fading smile, Anna crossed the street and I turned to find Elena watching me.

'She seems *nice*. Why did she ask if life was back to normal?'

'Oh, I had a few problems and Anna helped me out. She's a solicitor,' I lied to add weight to my explanation. 'It was before we were going out.' That extra information didn't help.

'Well, she looked *very* pleased to see you.'

'Really? I don't think so. She's just like that.'

'Hmm… I'll give you a call later to see how you are. Although you seem a lot brighter. Perhaps a night out of the office is all you need.'

'If I don't get some rest, I'll have a migraine from hell for days.' It sounded like the sort of thing people who get migraines said. I also needed an excuse not to answer the phone when she checked on me. Having my own telephone wasn't always a plus.

'Okay. Make sure you look after yourself. And no drinking!'

After a long kiss, I descended into the underground.

From the street, Primrose House looked like a smart hotel, but inside the décor was cream and basic. I found the desk unmanned, and as I peered down the corridor for signs of life, a woman's voice came from an office behind reception. The plastic plaque on her door said 'Manager'. She craned her head around to see me, and with the phone receiver wedged under her chin, mouthed that she'd be a minute. She came out after three.

'Hello, I'm Mr Webster. I'm—'

'Oh, Mr Webster. You found us then.'

'Yes—'

The phone rang again. 'One second.' She took it at reception. 'Good evening, Primrose House. Can you hold on a moment, please?' She threw her head towards the corridor. 'Tara!' A red-headed girl in a yellow nursing uniform appeared from a doorway. 'Tara, can you take Mr Webster through to Mrs Featherstone, please?' She went back to her call.

'Yes, of course. Follow me, please, Mr Webster.'

'Thank you,' I said to the manager, even though I'd lost her attention. I followed Tara along the corridor, past a lounge where several people sat listening to old-time music, and to a door with a gold number four. Tara knocked once and then walked straight in.

We entered a fair-sized room with a bed surrounded by built-in cupboards and two armchairs that pointed towards a deafening television. As we drew near to the chairs, a crumpled old woman came into view. She was wearing a lemon flowery dress and brown, slip-on shoes. Her skin hung loose from her bare arms and tufts of pure-white hair scarcely covered her skull. She was beyond any scale of recognition.

'Faye, you have a visitor.' Tara touched her arm. 'Faye?'

The old lady looked up through watery eyes. 'Yes?'

'You have a visitor.'

'Edward?'

'No, a nice Mr Webster has come.' Tara turned to me. 'Do you want to move closer, so she can see you?'

'Hello, Faye, it's Peter.' I forgot myself and gave my real name. Faye didn't care who I was; she had other things on her mind.

'Can you turn that television off? I hate the blasted thing, but they keep turning it on.'

Tara laughed. 'Yes, we're here to make your life as miserable as possible, Faye.' She winked at me and pressed the remote. 'I'll leave you two to have a chat. Would you like tea, Peter?'

'No, thank you, I'll be fine.'

'I'll bring your cocoa in a bit, Faye.' She closed the door as she left.

Faye stared in my direction, but I sensed that she wasn't really looking. Her mouth formed silent words and I wondered whether she'd already forgotten I was there. I was just about to speak when she surprised me.

'Does Edward know about the boy?' She wiped her mouth with an embroidered hanky.

'Do you mean Ned?' Her eyes betrayed nothing, and I wondered how connected she was to the outside world. 'His son?'

I waited, but she fell silent.

'Do you mean his son?' I prompted.

'His son!' She shook her head and tutted. 'Well, it's too late now, isn't it?'

'Too late for what?' She didn't answer. 'Faye? Too late for what?'

The old lady closed her eyes and bowed her head. A few moments later, she puffed out noisy sleeping breaths. I watched her for a while as a clock in the corridor chimed the half hour and the place carried on with life. Someone switched on a television in the neighbouring room, and I could hear one of the carers giving out cups of tea and cocoa.

Faye lifted her head again. 'Hello? You're not getting me in that bath tonight. You'd better go.'

'Faye, you were telling me about Edward.'

'Edward? Edward is dead, you silly man.'

'I know—'

'I want you to go now.'

Faye bowed her head again.

After sitting for several long minutes, I gave up and left.

I walked to gather my thoughts, sensing something very wrong with the whole business. When I passed Gloucester Road tube station, for a moment I considered catching up with Elena in the pub. I could feel my energy reserves sinking, though, and rather than push them, I went home.

My mind stuck on it. I tried to sleep but found myself thinking of Faye. How had she visited my room that night? The likeness with the painting was irrefutable. And why ask whether Edward knows about the boy? What should he have known? And Michael's dreams of the woman trying to find me... it all went around and around in my head until I drifted and replayed Margaret's true story of *The Silent Accusation*.

Then it dawned on me and I sat up with the shock. The book was holding a different key.

I'd given Edward's notebook to George Locke, but somewhere, I still had my pad. I climbed out of bed, went to the bags in the lounge and found the contents of the sideboard. I rummaged around until I spotted the familiar cardboard cover of the pad and flicked through the pages of notes. '...*seduced the housekeeper Dorothy... shared a bed under Faye's nose... jumped out of his bedroom window and was found by Mrs Talbert.*'

The next morning, I called Helen and told her my migraine was worse. I then caught the tube to Holborn. Entering the Record Office's double doors, I cast a hopeful eye around for Jean, but the place was virtually empty.

Like a pro, I walked straight to the deaths section and located the register. I opened it out onto the wooden bench table and this time noted the details – Daniel Featherstone, February 1982, aged forty-four. Then, in the births section, I searched three volumes until I found him.

THIRTY-SIX

With the house on the market, I needed to get in there fast and before a surveyor poked around. I left the Records Office and called James from a phone box to ask who was handling the sale. He didn't know, so my next trip was to the house to check the agent's board. I then called Frederick Percy and Sons, hoping to get the key. There my luck ran out. All viewings were during prearranged open days, and I'd just missed one that morning.

'Oh, that's a shame,' I said. 'I've been viewing houses in London for a few days, and I've only just seen this one. I'm going back to Bristol tomorrow and was hoping to look around in the morning before my train. Is there any chance that you could make an exception and let me have the key?'

'I don't think—'

'I'm a cash buyer and need a quick purchase.'

'Cash buyer, did you say?'

'Yes.'

'Well, under the circumstances, let me see what we can do. Can you hold for a minute?' I waited, feeling confident. 'Thanks for holding, but I've got bad news. After today's viewing, someone made an offer, which the vendor has just accepted. Sorry about that.'

'So, I can't look?'

'No, I'm afraid not.'

'But if the offer has only just been accepted... I may offer more.'

'I understand, but it doesn't work like that. When an offer is accepted, the property is withdrawn from the market with no further viewings.'

'What, no exceptions?'

'No, sorry.'

I hung up, frustrated at missing my chance.

THIRTY-SEVEN

It was a mild, dry night with a near-full moon. Pretty good for October. I left my flat just after midnight, my rucksack laden with David's left-behind tools. To keep my cover, I caught a taxi, got out on the adjacent street and then walked to the back of number fifteen.

The gate swung easily on its hinges, as if it knew not to make a peep. I shone the torch down the empty path, which also lit up its borders. I had found the roses. They were overgrown and adorned with dead, brown heads. Faye's splendid garden lay tangled and neglected.

As I swept the torch back, a tablet of stone in the flowerbed caught my eye. There was an image carved on it and I walked over to look. My legs went weak. It was a pentagram overlaid with the devil's face. I recoiled with the shock of it. Was this black magic after all? I felt a thousand miles out of my depth.

With my legs still wobbly, I stood for a moment, steadying my nerves. If I was going to do this, I knew I couldn't be defeated by a silly lump of stone. I pulled myself together and pushed on down the path to the back door. This time it was tight in its frame, and when I pressed my body against it, it didn't move. The upper frosted-glass panel offered the best route of attack. I put down the torch and spade, swung off my rucksack and rummaged for the hammer. Muting the glass with the bag, I tapped at the panel, and it tinkled into pieces. I stopped and listened for anyone investigating the noise and, with the all-clear, levered my body up through the door remains and into the kitchen.

The inside of the house felt no safer than the garden: it was alive with shadows and ominously dank. I panned the torch around, looking for clues and something I'd missed before. The beam found the route I had taken to the first floor and then revealed the door going under those stairs. Of course, there it was, unexplored and forgotten. I tiptoed over, my heart thumping, my nerves alive with expectation. I turned the knob and, holding my breath, drew open the door.

Thick, damp air caught the back of my throat and my eyes fixed on a set of narrow, concrete steps that disappeared into a black abyss. Feeling through tacky cobwebs, I found an old, stick-type light switch, and at its snap, a naked bulb woke. Hopeful, I looked back down the steps. Darkness overpowered and devoured the weak light. I stared, listening for terrors that were yet to stir, as they waited for me to come.

Every fibre of my body screamed against going down, but I crept, stair by stair, until I reached the bottom step, where the dark almost swallowed the light from my torch. Uneasy, I searched for another switch and thanked God when I struck one and a yellow light blinked on. The scene wasn't what I expected.

The cellar was about ten by eight feet with brick walls and a concrete floor. Metal racks held old bottles and boxes of jumble, their cardboard black with mould. The floor was a smooth, solid surface, and no ordinary spade would release what lay beneath. Stumped, I searched around the walls with my torch, but they also gave nothing away. Then the cellar door creaked.

'Fuck this.' I raced up the cellar steps, two by two, and burst into the kitchen. I darted the torch around the room but caught nothing in its beam. Then I heard another creak, upstairs, above my head and remembered my last visit's intruder.

'Hello?' I shouted up the basement stairs. 'Who's there?'

Nothing came back and I knew that no physical person was calling. Taking a deep breath, I walked up the stairs to the hall.

Once again, the front-door fanlight came to my rescue, and I orientated my senses in its glow. Then another creak sounded, another floor up. Something was drawing me in.

I edged to the foot of the main staircase and forced myself to shine the torch up. There were no visible demons. I put my foot on the stair but lost my nerve and stepped off. I hung there for what seemed like an age. Then, with a push, I climbed.

Each stair creaked to signal my progress to anyone lying in wait. Against the drumming of my heart, I tread feather-light as my eyeline became level with the first floor. Through the banister, a landing with five closed doors emerged. I conquered the top stair and assessed my choices of hidden rooms.

I moved to the closest door to my right. I walked over on eggshells and lifted my hand to the knob. At that moment came another creak.

'Hello?'

My heart stopped at a scratching sound. It was my shoulder brushing against the wall and I let out a puff of relief. I flicked the torch around, just in case, and reassured, turned back to the door. I curled my fingers around the knob and twisted and paused, preparing myself for the scene.

With a loud, complaining creak, the door swung wide on its hinges, revealing an empty room. The beam illuminated patterned wallpaper and a thin carpet that fell short of the skirting by two or three inches. The black mouth of a fire surround glowered from the chimney breast.

I crossed the threshold without risking switching on the light. Something dropped in front of my face, and I yelped and jumped back. It was only a spider, dancing on its thread.

And then I smelt it, as clear as anything, the scent of roses. And I knew I was in the right place. Somewhere in this room, the answer lay.

I followed the torch beam around the walls and was just about to step when I heard a sound. I listened hard as the volume grew. My ears screamed in denial and my heart almost burst from my chest. The scraping sound crept from behind me, inching closer and closer, growing in strength. I cowered, trembling, praying to be saved.

Then a hand grabbed my ankle.

I reeled back shrieking, falling and dropping the torch. I paddled away for my life, then scampered to my feet and lunged for the light switch.

With the strike of the light my tormentor had vanished.

For a split second, I was out of there, darting for the door. But with my hand on the doorframe, I stopped. I'd come too far to abandon this. I took two deep breaths, to steady my heart, and turned to face my fate.

I stood, rooted to my safe spot, and looked at the age-stained wallpaper. I moved my gaze to the fireplace – there was something in the grate. I started towards it but then a floorboard creaked. I stopped dead at the sound of it. I rocked, stepping off and then on the board, just to confirm the sound.

I walked over to the corner of the carpet and curled it back to form a loop. The limp material rolled clumsily over the floor, revealing the long-hidden boards. There was a patch in the middle where the boards had been cut through and replaced with nails instead of tacks.

Dropping my rucksack like a stone, I peered inside for the claw hammer and unhooked it from the tangle of tools. The claw barely fit into the gap, and when I tried to prise the boards, the angle wouldn't let me. I grabbed a flat chisel to slot into the edge and raised the board high enough to slip in the claw. When I pushed hard, a slim piece of wood fractured away, sending me off balance. 'Shit,' I cursed, and steadied myself. Using the gap created, I managed to get a hold to lever up the board in fierce jerks and pushes. The board unwillingly surrendered, its nails screaming as it gave up its secret, rising just enough for me to pull it free with my hands.

Peering down, I wasn't sure, so I moved to the next board. With a combination of hammer levers and hand tugs, I lifted that too. I could see something – a bundle, a shape wrapped in a cloth. My hand reached out and picked up a corner of the fragile, ageing material. Shaking, I peeled it back and shrieked.

Hollow eyes and yellow teeth grinned through the gap in the floor.

THIRTY-EIGHT

I made it home, but not to bed. I was too agitated, too high. My mind played and replayed the horror of revealing that terrible face. It felt familiar, and something stirred deep.

At work I get the call. It's Sarah.

'Mum's been rushed into hospital, West Middlesex. She collapsed in the street and they think it's a heart attack.'

'Oh, fuck. I'm on my way.'

By the time I burst into A&E, Mum's in the operating theatre. A nurse leads me round to where Dad is waiting. He stands in his golf clothes, his ashen face aged ten years and tears streaming down his cheeks. He's horrified that I've found him in that state. I walk to him, but he turns towards the orange plastic chairs.

'David should be here in a minute.' He sniffs and sits. 'He said he would come straight away.'

'Okay,' I say, because there's nothing more to add. I add nothing.

I want to take a chair but don't feel welcome to sit near him, and so I stand. As I look across the waiting room, I notice the doctor approach. Dad doesn't register the look that's in her eyes, but I know it straight away.

'Mr Tyler, is it?' Dad nods, hope betraying his composure. 'I'm afraid I have bad news.'

And then my world collapses. My gentle protector gone.

Yet I am the one with him, standing alongside him, at the very moment he needs it. And that must count for something.

I move to put my hand on his shoulder. I'm shocked as he takes it and holds it.

The doctor says several things that I don't hear because I'm screaming at myself not to break down.

Then Dad interrupts. 'I want to see her.'

'Yes, of course. I'll ask the nurse.'

'My son will be here soon. I'd like him to be with me.'

The doctor looks at me and then back at Dad. 'Whenever you're ready, Mr Tyler.'

I ignore the wounding. 'Dad, I should call Sarah.'

'Oh, heavens, poor Sarah. Of course, let her know.'

I go off to make the call, leaving him to wait for David. I get Adam because Sarah's already on her way, unknowing.

When I return to Dad, he's agitated, still waiting for David. I live every second of five excruciating minutes, and then the nurse comes.

'Are you ready, Mr Tyler?' She looks to me as the man in charge and I look at Dad.

'I suppose so,' he says, lost and broken. We go with the nurse.

She leads us into a private room with a screen around a trolley bed. We go behind the screen and there's the shape of a body covered in a white sheet. The nurse takes the corner of the sheet and peels it back. In slow motion, the ghastly, unprettied face of my mother is revealed. It's too much for Dad to take and he disintegrates into giant sobs. The nurse nods respectfully and leaves.

213

'She looks awful.' He weeps.

'She's been through a trauma. She's at peace now, though.' I wasn't faring any better but was proud of myself for holding it together, outdoing my iron-man father.

'You weakened her heart when she had you. She was never the same. The doctors told her. She was too stubborn and wouldn't listen.' He shakes his head. 'It ruined our lives. I told her to get rid of it.'

I stare, horrified, not believing my ears. 'You're talking about *me*?'

He keeps his eyes fixed on my mother. He doesn't care; he has no shame for what he has said, not even at her deathbed. I fight back tears and clear my throat, but then David walks in.

'David! Thank God.' Dad crumples into David's square body. The point of my existence is gone.

THIRTY-NINE

After sitting up for the rest of the night, waiting for the morning to begin, I was out of the door and travelling by seven. I needed to straighten things out, before I called the police.

'Oh, hello, Mr… Webster. What a surprise to see you again so soon.' The manager checked her watch. 'And so early.'

'I wanted to pop in on my way to work. You don't mind, do you?'

'Sorry, but I know that I mentioned this. No visits before nine o'clock.'

'I'm sure you could make an exception.' I saw that my assumption needled her.

'We do this to ensure the residents' safety.'

'Honestly, I understand. I would never normally ask, but I have some very important business.'

'With Faye? Something that can't wait 'til later?'

'It really needs to be now.'

She stared, annoyed at being undermined and suspicious of my motives. 'I'll see what I can do.'

She went into her office and before long she was back. 'There's no one free to take you down – they're all getting people ready. It's our busiest time, Mr Webster.' She was locked into making her point.

'It's okay, I'll wait.' That didn't suit her either, but she shrugged and walked away. Frustrated, I sat in the waiting area and picked up a copy of *Ideal Home*. I'd only reached the contents page when she reappeared with news.

'I've just spoken to a one of the carers. Faye doesn't want an early visit. She's usually better after lunch. I'm sorry, but I tried.'

'I suppose I'll have to come back then.'

'Yes, as I thought.'

'Perhaps around two?'

'That would work fine.' She returned to the office, her victory giving a spring to her step. The mighty manager's games of self-importance had upset my plans.

Then I had an idea.

I opened and shut the front door but stayed on the inside. I watched to make sure it was safe – she was too full of herself to see my deception – and then made a dash down the corridor.

Ahead of me, Tara came out of another room, and I feared I was done for. I froze as I watched her reorganise a trolley of medicines. I was considering turning back when she set off in the opposite direction. Riding my luck, I crept, following Tara, until I reached Faye's door and slunk in.

Contrary to the manager's misgivings, the old woman looked perfectly alert. She was sat in her chair, wrapped in her dressing gown and humming to the radio tunelessly. I sat down opposite and waited for her acknowledgement, but an inner sense advised her otherwise. So, I went ahead anyway.

'Hello, Faye.' She stared out with vacant eyes. 'Or should I call you Mrs Talbert?' I waited for a reaction that didn't come. 'Except, I doubt that you were ever a Mrs?'

'It must have been hard watching Edward go out of his mind for a woman he couldn't find, while you offered him love that he didn't want.

'And then when he died, you faced a life of hardship with his unborn son. Without Edward to protect you, was Faye finally going to cast you out?'

More silence.

'Well, I've found her and I'm going to the police. It'll be in their hands soon.'

She turned her head, looked directly into my eyes and whispered, 'George will not let you do that.'

'George? Who's George? ...You don't mean George Locke?'

She smiled a vicious sneer and with that she was gone again, humming in a trance.

'Faye!' I shook her arm, but she was unreachable. 'Mrs Talbert? I want you to tell me who George is.'

'Oh, you'll not get much sense out of her.' I turned and saw Tara carrying in clean sheets, unfazed at my presence. 'She'll be like that for a while, I should imagine.'

I looked again at the old woman and wondered how much she really knew about what was happening. I guessed that it was more than she let on.

'I should get going anyway.'

Tara started to strip the bed. 'See you again soon.'

I left her to it and made my way back towards reception, peeking to check that the coast was clear before escaping through the doors. I walked to Kensington tube and jumped on the circle line, my head filled with working out how George might be linked to Mrs Talbert.

The distraction almost derailed my morning as I needed to deal with Faye's body before an unsuspecting estate agent or buyer got a shock. I called the police from a phone box

217

near to the office. There was no way to explain what I'd done or why, so I just gave an anonymous tip-off, saying enough to ensure that they would go out to the house and find Faye's remains.

Closing the phone box, I stared at Montgomery's. The door to sanity stood merely a few yards away. I lingered, weighing it up, and, realising that a normal day was a fantasy, I went instead to find George.

The same young woman sat at Locke and Noble's reception.

'Is it possible to contact George Locke, please?'

'What is it about?' she asked.

'It's about his recently deceased client, Ned Clayton. George will definitely want to speak to me.'

My confidence carried through and she asked me to take a seat while she made a call. After a few minutes, she ushered me towards the office where I'd spent that afternoon with George in what felt like another lifetime. I walked in and George sat waiting in one of the chairs, this time in front of a cold, dead fire.

'Peter! How nice to see you.'

'I'm here on unfortunate business.'

'Oh.' He raised an eyebrow.

'I've just found Faye's dead body.'

'*What?!*' He genuinely looked astonished.

'I know. It's rather shocking. But Mrs Talbert seems to think you know all about it.'

'Me? Oh no, absolutely not.'

'I called the police—'

'What did you tell them?' He'd given the game away and my anger rose.

'Well, there'll be no skeletons in closets, or should I say under floorboards, by the time they've finished.'

'Did you tell them that I knew about it?'

'Knew what?'

'No, I mean—'

'I wanted to give you the opportunity to explain before I said anything to the police.'

'I see.' Finally defeated, he stared into the empty fire.

'Nothing to say then?'

'Peter, come and sit down.'

'No, I'm happy here. Faye has been murdered by someone you seem to be protecting. And now it makes sense why you were so interested about what else I'd found in the house. And why you weren't surprised that someone had beaten me to it. You sent them, didn't you? You were trying to cover your tracks. That's why they were there in the house.'

'Peter! Stop! I know nothing about Faye. Well...' he looked away, 'not quite nothing. *Please*, sit down!'

I sat.

'When James asked me about the house deeds, I knew it meant trouble. I had forgotten all about the blasted things. James, on the other hand, was delighted to have heard from Faye. Of course, I didn't let on that it wasn't her.

'After Edward's death, Faye was a broken woman. I was shocked to see how much she still cared for him, after all the suffering he had inflicted on her. Yet Edward was still the love of her life, and she was devasted.

'I found some photographs of Edward that I thought Faye would like. So, one evening, I called round.' He shifted in his chair. 'She was a *very* attractive woman... a woman with needs, who had been alone for... too long. I am sure you can work out the details.

'Just that one slip, and that wretched housekeeper discovered us. And then it all tumbled like an avalanche.

Faye thought that she wanted me, *needed* me. She was out of her mind with grief and... *dangerous*. What happened between us – that slip, that was all it was, I swear, a slip – it meant so much more to her. She was going to tell my wife. It was only one night, for heaven's sake! We were not in love – I was not going to destroy my family, my business, my life, for one tiny indiscretion. Hell, what man would?

'Then, whilst I was dealing with that, Dorothy, the housekeeper, announced she was pregnant. Another illegitimate child of Edward's to torment Faye. And Faye was determined to turn her out onto the street. But Dorothy had other ideas. She claimed she could prove that Edward had provided for her. Knowing my profession, Dorothy came after me, demanding my help – or else!

'She gave me no choice in the matter. She put a proposal to me. She would deal with my problem with Faye, as long as I kept silent and allowed *her* to live in the house. She insisted it was what Edward had wanted – to provide for his unborn child. Given the way Edward had searched for Ned, of course he would have looked after this baby. It was all very easy for me to believe, and I thought my conscience was clear.'

'So, you agreed to get *rid* of Faye?'

'No! Not like that. I had no idea! I thought...' He glanced at me and then looked away. 'I chose not to think. I panicked... and was desperate to make it all go away. I didn't ask what she had in mind. I didn't want to know. The more I knew, the more I was involved. I thought it would be some sort of blackmail, like she was blackmailing me. Living with Faye for all those years, I figured that Dorothy knew all sorts of useful things. Blackmail for sure, never murder, for pity's sake!'

'And you turned a blind eye, while she took Faye's identity and they lived as Edward's widow and son.'

'Yes, I did.' He hung his head. 'I held the separate trust for Ned. At least I made sure that he was not affected by it all.'

'At *least*. You've chosen the right word there.'

George looked crestfallen, absorbing my words before carrying on. 'When I heard that her son, Daniel, had died, I kept a close eye. Dorothy was already frail, and I knew that losing Daniel would send her over the edge and probably into care. When they emptied the house, I saw a chance. Shameful, I know, but I needed to check that nothing could uncover my actions, after all my efforts to hide them.

'And that's when *you* turned up at the house, curse the gods. And not only to the house but then to my very own practice! When James told me, I nearly fell off my chair. And of course, I made sure that I spoke to you myself.

'But that business with Ned was truly terrible. You must believe me, I was desperate to put everything right for Edward. I have lived with the guilt for years. Decades of it eating away at me like a cancer. I *needed* this chance to make amends and find what little peace I could.'

'Unbelievable. This is such a mess.' Exhausted and broken, I rubbed my eyes.

'*Please*, Peter. What is done is done. How will it help anyone if it comes out now? All it will do is destroy more lives.'

'*Yours,* you mean.'

'No. Mine was destroyed long ago. I mean the lives of my sons and grandchildren. Innocent, good people like James. You wouldn't want to ruin his reputation, would you?'

I glared, livid at the blackmail.

'I *swear* to you, Peter, I had no hand in Faye's death.'

'Yes, you did.'

'That *woman*, she had already decided. Faye's fate was as good as sealed when Edward killed himself. Look at

221

me! What good will come of destroying my family over something that happened forty years ago? I am an old man. My miserable life is nearly over. It's only innocent people who will suffer.'

'I've heard enough.'

And with that I got up and walked out, determined not to put George's mind to rest.

With the enormity of it all preying on my mind, the journey home passed in a daze. I'd suffered Ned's suicide, found a dead body and uncovered a murderer – all due to one random act of taking a book.

Did I want to take George on too? After all, what proof did I have? It would be my word against his. He was a respectable solicitor, with a reputation that stretched through generations and the resources of one of the best law firms in London behind him. I was a 'greedy stockbroker' who had recently cracked up.

Then my mind switched to Faye and her wretched life. The love of her life had been a cruel and calculated cheat. He'd left her at the mercy of her own housekeeper, a woman carrying his child from another affair. Then finally, after finding a little comfort with George, she'd suffered the ultimate betrayal by him.

And of course, the hauntings. They'd been her all along. She'd reached out across the ether, not to point me towards Ned but for me to find the house, the story and her wronged body.

I reached home and savoured closing my door on the world. Exhausted, I threw myself on the sofa. A fiery red autumn sun poured in through the windows and, with my eyes closed, I basked in its rays. And then came the familiar scent, strong and sweet. I opened my eyes and there, on the table, was a perfect, crimson-red rose.

I blinked and stared hard, checking I wasn't seeing things. Amazed, I picked it up, holding it gently by the stem. As I drew in its heady smell, a woman's voice whispered, 'Thank you.'

FORTY

My luck changed instantly. I caught the tube train I ran for, stepped indoors before a downpour and found ten pounds on the street. By chance, I glanced at the paper and caught an excellent investment.

When Saturday morning came, I noticed how fresh the rose still looked. I'd put it on the windowsill, in a glass, and over a week later, it looked new. Mentally thanking Faye for my good-luck charm, I bent to smell it just as the phone rang.

'Peter, I'm so glad I've caught you.' It was Philip. 'Can you get over here?'

'Have I done something wrong?'

'No. It's the account I signed over to Ajay. Bill McKenzie isn't happy and is coming at five to discuss. I can't get hold of Ajay for love nor money. But I can't wait for him. I promised McKenzie a full review and plan. Peter, I need you. You know the account.'

I rearranged plans with Elena and scooted over to the office. Philip was already knee deep in figures when I arrived. He moved aside, biting his thumbnail as I read through his work, desperate to start the next stage. And that's how we continued all afternoon – him offering ideas, eager for my judgement, and me refining and shaping our attack.

While I finished the proposal, he made coffee. He carried in two mugs. 'I'm so grateful to you. I'd let go of this and… I made a mistake. I placed too much trust in Ajay.'

'Ajay is good.'

'Don't let me off the hook. I was pissed off with you and was rubbing it in. I've not been fair. Yet here you are now, saving my neck.

'And I'm going to show you how much I *do* value you. But for now, show me what you've done, and it better be good!' He slapped me on the back and I gathered my notes.

After I'd pitched to him, he insisted that I led the meeting. Everything went to plan. Bill McKenzie was impressed and by the time he'd left, I'd been elevated to superhero.

Back in the office on Monday, Ajay was notably subdued, while Philip crowed about me in a way that even I found sickening. Instead of being my usual modest self, I knocked Ajay back into place with a few sharp quips about his priorities. *All in good sport, old chum.*

On Friday morning, Sarah called.

'What have you been up to?' she asked as if nothing had happened.

'The usual stuff. Work, of course.'

'That makes a change.'

'Things are going really well again. I should get that promotion back in a couple of months.'

'I knew you would.'

'And I'm going out with Elena, one of the analysts.'

'You have been busy! What's she like?'

'Crazy, but in a good way. At least she's not Anna, I suppose.'

'Don't be like that. I was out of my mind with worry for Michael. That's why I've called. He's been so much better lately. His bad dreams seem to have gone and he's like a different boy. Yesterday, he wanted to talk about it. He insisted that you weren't to blame for any of this. Whatever has happened to Michael, I know it wasn't your fault.'

'I can't believe you thought that I could hurt him.'

'Of course you wouldn't. Not intentionally. I just didn't know whether this had anything to do with... you know...'

'That was a long time ago, I was a child.'

'Yes, like Michael. Look, I don't want to start all that. Michael feels bad that we've fallen out and blames himself. I can't have him thinking that. I want you to come and see us so that we can put things right. Will you?' My relief was tempered by hurt. 'Will you come and bring Elena? We'd love to meet her.'

'Well... she might like that, I suppose.'

'I should never have said those things to you. I overreacted.'

'It's okay, I understand.'

'You know I love you, don't you?'

I was too choked to respond.

'Please, come and see me.'

'I will. I'll come soon.'

FORTY-ONE

Elena came round on Saturday afternoon. When she arrived, I could hardly get a word out of her. I feared that I'd done something wrong, that her patience with work had finally run out, but she was oddly clingy too.

'By the way, Sarah called yesterday.' I tried to raise some interest.

'Sarah?'

'My sister. She wants us to go over and stay.' She showed no enthusiasm. 'I told her about us and she's keen to meet you. They have a farm in Norfolk. It's a great place to relax and do stuff like walking, reading, drinking. You like drinking right?' Still nothing. 'I thought we could go in a couple of weeks?'

'Yes, okay.'

Confused and deciding not to push it, I left her to her thoughts and made coffee. When I held the mug towards her, she was miles away.

'Elena, what's wrong?'

She looked up and took the drink. 'Peter... We need to talk.'

Oh, it's over, I thought, and dreaded the next words. Yes,

I'd been spending too much time with my wife, Philip. I sat next to her and she took my hand, rubbing her thumb into my palm and resting her head against mine.

'I'm pregnant.'

'What?' I sat forward.

'That's where I was yesterday afternoon.'

'*Pregnant?!*'

'I know it's—'

'You said you were on the pill.'

'I was. I am! I mean… of course I was. I don't know why it's happened.'

'Shit.'

'Oh, thanks.'

'Fuck. I don't know what to say. It's a shock.' Elena's chin wobbled and then the tears came. Silently they streamed down her cheeks as she wiped them away. 'Elena…' I put my arm around her, drawing her close. 'Look… I just… I'm sorry.'

'I didn't plan this either,' she said between sobs. 'I don't know what I'm going to do. I need you to help me.'

'Okay.'

'You really don't want this. And neither do I. Not this way. But I definitely can't get rid of it.' Elena's family were devout Catholics. This was serious.

'No, I don't want you to do that.' The memory of my father's revelation, his preference to kill me prebirth, stabbed. 'I just need to think… It's a shock.'

'It was a shock for me too.'

'Hey, I'm sorry. Come here.' I cocooned her in a tight hug. 'I just need to think it through.'

'I am sorry. I didn't want this to happen.'

We sat hugging, the plastic kitchen wall clock ticking through the vacuum of my thoughts. This would take some working out.

'I think it's a boy.' Her words drew me back.

'You don't know.'

'I can't get the image of a little Peter Junior out of my head.' She expelled a heavy sigh of a laugh.

'Poor him.'

'Don't say that, you're lovely.' *Lovely?* Was that the best I could do? 'Don't look at me like that, you are.' She traced her finger over my knuckle and then took my hand. 'Here, Peter Junior, meet your daddy.' The word daddy twitched my insides as she placed my hand flat on her stomach. I rubbed her belly over her dress, making wider and wider circles. Then she caught my hand, pushed it downwards and, with her other arm, hooked my neck and drew me to her lips. We kissed, pressing together, the charge in our bodies electrifying the moment.

Elena half-undressed me, tugging at my belt and forcing down my jeans. I attempted to undo her dress, but she pulled it over her head before I could manage it. Our lovemaking was fiery, making up for unfound words and raw emotions, and afterwards, we both lay quiet on the sofa.

I traced my fingers across her pale, flat belly and mused, 'Isn't it strange to think that there's a little person in there?'

'Believe me, it feels more than strange. Although…'

'Hmm?'

'It kind of makes me feel… warm. Proud. Oh, I don't know what I mean. It's weird.'

'I hope he doesn't have your ears.'

'Very funny!' She thumped my arm. 'He'll be gorgeous, and everyone will love him.'

'An Italian Romeo?'

'Maybe. A handsome actor or racing driver.'

'He's going to be a bloody lawyer, like his grandfather's father's father before him. It's compulsory. Only the very special get to do something else.'

'Or the misfits.'

Ouch! 'Yeah, well, I might just let him be a millionaire playboy all his life. That'd jazz up the Tyler legacy.' A new thought that I'd beaten David to popping out Tylers amused me.

'He'll follow the more respectable family line and work for his grandfather's business.'

'Eh? Oh, your dad.'

Elena fell lost in thought.

'What's wrong?'

'You haven't even met Papà yet, and when you do—'

'It's okay, don't worry about that now.'

'But I do. I can't stop thinking about it. I want him to like you… I don't want him to meet you like this.'

'It'll be fine, we'll sort it.' I cradled her and kissed the top of her head.

'So… you might want this baby?'

'Do you?' That wasn't the answer she wanted, and I hated seeing her face fall. 'I've got big, big plans for my boy.'

'What if I'm wrong and it's a girl?'

'Then you're on your own.'

'What?!' she squealed.

I grabbed and tickled her, and she tickled me back. 'Stop! Stop!' I cried. 'I need to pee.'

'Spoilsport.' She released her grip. 'Don't be long!'

As I walked to the bathroom, I realised that, beyond the shock, I felt happy. There would be a new life in the world thanks to me, taking me from youngest child to daddy in a matter of months, and I was actually happy. But could I really make a go of things with Elena? Could I disrupt my career, just as things were taking off again, to become a dad? Well, I was damn sure that I was going to do a better job than my own father. I'd give my son confidence. I'd show him love. I'd give him attention and support – whatever he needed.

I left the bathroom and saw Elena gazing across the room with an odd expression. 'Who gave you the rose?'

There was absolute silence while my mind said, *Oh, fuck.*

'It's that fucking Anna, isn't it?'

'No, Elena, it isn't. I wasn't sure what to say because… I feel such a prat.'

'Don't fuck me around, not now.'

'Here, it's for you. I meant to give it to you when I came round last Sunday, and I completely forgot. Do you really think I'd keep a rose from another woman in my flat, right under your nose?'

'I suppose that would be dim, even for you. Where's the other eleven then, cheapskate?'

'I was being romantic. I wanted to serenade you.' I took the rose out of the glass and, putting it between my teeth, went down on one knee. 'Ow, shit.'

'What've you done?'

'A thorn.' I stood up, dabbing my lip with the back of my hand.

'You're bleeding, here…' She pressed on a tissue. 'That's divine justice for making me jealous.'

I pushed an image of Faye out of my mind. 'I'll be alright.'

When the bleeding stopped, it left a hangover of soreness and swelling. I figured I deserved it for lying.

The day was tainted with a strange atmosphere. I'd planned to take Elena out to dinner, but she wasn't up to it, so I popped out to collect pizza and wine. Elena decided to stay over, and we talked more about the baby. However, several times, I caught her distracted and staring glassy-eyed into space, trying to come to terms with her unplanned new life.

On Sunday morning, Elena cooked bacon while I read the paper. The rose caught my eye and I saw that a petal had dropped. A sickening feeling stabbed in the pit of my stomach, the anxiety that soon, my new-found good fortune might die too. I reached for the petal just as Elena cried out in the kitchen.

I rushed in. 'Are you okay?'

'No, I've burned myself.'

'You need more practice.'

'Thanks.' She turned to run her hand under the tap.

'Here, let's have a look.' I took her hand. 'Bloody hell, how'd you do that?' A blistering welt bubbled up before my eyes.

'I'm not sure – it happened so fast and hurt so much. I looked away for a second and… I must have knocked the side of the pan with my hand.'

Just then the phone rang, and I left Elena to it while I answered. As I replaced the receiver, she came out from the kitchen.

'Who was it?'

'Philip.'

'And he wants you to go in?'

'Yes.'

'Great!'

'I can tell him no.'

'Not likely. You'll need to go. How long will you be?'

'Probably a while. We'll definitely do the cinema or something later, though.'

'It's okay. I'll stay here and read, and, to be frank, do some tidying up. You've turned a luxury flat into a pigsty. Everything will be nice and fresh when you get back, including me.' She walked over and we kissed.

On my way out, I looked again at the rose. Another petal had dropped. I walked over and bowed to smell it.

Its scent was still strong, filling my senses with a strange confidence. I needed to preserve the flower before it was too late. I decided to ask Elena how to do that, later.

Philip sat in a mountain of files, barely raising his eyes when I walked in. I waited until he was ready to share the urgency, but it never came. It soon became obvious that he didn't really need me; he just wanted me there while he prepared to meet the rest of the board. This was straightforward stuff for Philip, especially with all the information he'd had from his teams. He was taking advantage again.

As the afternoon ticked into evening, I kept sneaking glances at the time.

'No good checking your watch, we'll be here for a while yet.' He'd already erased last week's triumph from his memory.

'I need to call Elena.' He released a general huff. 'She'll want me home.'

I went across to my office and called her.

'Sorry, I think he plans to keep me here all night.'

'You're still in the office? Seems excessive, even for you.'

'Don't start. I'm with the gorgeous Philip and no one else. I'd put him on the phone, but he's hardly speaking a word.'

'That's convenient.'

'Look, I better go. Don't wait up if it gets late. I'll understand if you decide to go home.'

'I'll think about it.'

I put down the phone and saw a future of justifying myself to a wife waiting at home. A wife with a baby. Suddenly, I was suffocating, feeling trapped. I just wasn't ready for it.

I returned to Philip's office, envying his freedom to work when he liked. I'd never noticed him calling his wife with excuses. We worked for another hour before he said I could go, but after talking to Elena, I wanted to stay longer. Around seven, I popped out for Chinese and a bottle Philip's favourite wine. We'd done all the figures for Monday but had decided to review a couple of high-value files.

It was after ten when I finally made my way home, feeling more than satisfied with my evening. I walked into the flat wondering whether Elena had left but found her asleep in my bed. I watched her for a few seconds, conflicted between feeling affection and annoyance at finding her in my space.

I went back out to the lounge for a nightcap and then quietly got ready for bed. I crawled into the warm covers, snaking my arm around Elena as she snuggled into my spoon. The smell of her hair and the curve of her soft, small body moved something deep, and I felt a wave of protectiveness for this fragile creature who was carrying my child.

How could I have wished her away? I thought. I pulled her in closer and within a few minutes, I'd joined her in sleep.

FORTY-TWO

I woke just before the alarm and left Elena to sleep longer. When I whispered goodbye, she stirred and gave me a soft, sloppy kiss that tingled my belly. I tucked her in, kissed her forehead and then tiptoed out of the room. In the lounge, I checked the rose: several fallen petals framed it. I needed to act fast and made a note to deal with it as soon as I got home.

Just before the board meeting, Philip marched over to my office.

'We used the wrong fucking figures.'

It took me a few seconds too long to follow him.

'We've prepared the board report on some complete nonsense.' I could see who was getting the blame in this 'we' relationship.

The best response eluded me: *'How did that happen...?'*, *'Can you work around it...?'*, *'Just tell the board we made a mistake...'* Every option was a fool's thought. In the end I just said, 'Shit, I'm sorry. Let me take a look.'

'I have thirty minutes. What the fuck can you do in thirty minutes?'

'I don't know, but let me try.'

'Do it then.' He threw the papers down and slammed my door.

Luckily, I spotted the mistake straight away. We'd swapped around two sets of figures in the final calculations and other than that, the work was solid. I had no time to re-write the final projector sheet, so I sketched out a brief for Philip to wing. It wasn't ideal, but when I took him through it, he mumbled a tepid thank-you.

Around eleven, I stretched my legs and looked for Elena. Viv, her manager, said she'd called in sick. I phoned home and found her trying to rouse herself. She felt too ill to talk, so I promised to leave early to be with her.

When I got home, Elena was slouched on the sofa, watching the news about serial killer Dennis Nilson.

'Looks gruesome.' I bent to kiss her. 'How you feeling?'

'Much better actually.'

'Is it the baby?'

'Morning sickness? I think so.'

'I missed you at work today. It's been a day from hell.' I dropped down next to her.

'What, for you? Golden boy? Spending all Sunday with your lover didn't do you much good then.'

'No. It's been a testing day. I don't want to think about it. Give me a hug.' We came together and being held felt good. My back ached and my head was full. Wondering if my lucky rose was wearing off, I glanced at it and my heart stopped.

'Where's the rose?'

'In the bin, I'm afraid.'

'Why?'

'It was dead. I know you like your money's worth, but they don't—'

'Which bin did you put it in?'

'Are you crazy?' She saw my face. 'I emptied all the bins. They were overflowing.'

'Why didn't you check with me first?'

'It was *my* rose. Or so you said.'

'I don't want all this. Stuff getting thrown out when I'm not here—'

'You are joking.'

'...having to justify why I have to work. And putting up with digs about seeing someone else. I don't want it!'

'Sounds like you just don't want me, full stop!'

'It's not that.'

'No. You want me, as long as it's nothing to commit to. As long as there's no baby. Is that it?'

'That's not what I said.'

'Say it and have done. You don't want this baby.'

'*Okay!* I don't want a baby right now!' Elena froze and I just couldn't help myself. 'Look, things were going really well for me. I was back to where I was before.'

'Before when? Before I got *myself* pregnant?'

'No—'

'Fuck you!' She marched over to her bag and stuffed her things into it. 'You really are a shit. All this for one dead rose, that was supposed to be mine anyway! You fucking liar.'

'You don't understand. There's more to this than the baby.'

'I'm sure there is. I'm obviously not the person to share it with. Perhaps I should ask *Anna*. I bet she knows *all* about it.'

'Elena...' She saw it in my face.

'I thought so! You know, I really thought you were better than this.' She grabbed her coat, stormed out and slammed the door.

I closed my eyes and drew in my breath, trying to recapture some calm. Outside I could hear pigeons on the

237

window ledge, their trills merging with the brum of traffic. The clock drummed away the seconds.

What was I thinking? What the hell have I done? I have Elena and a baby. Isn't that more important than anything?

Then a noise invaded the air – a screech slicing the atmosphere for too many seconds, before exploding into a smash.

'Shit, Elena!' I ran to the window and, in the dark night, saw people rushing towards something just out of view. And for a few sick moments, the panic choked my breath. But then I saw Elena, on the pavement opposite, waving up at me.

'Oh, thank God.' I waved back to signal that I was on my way down, but Elena turned and walked away. 'She thought it was a wave goodbye,' I said to the empty room, and watched her turn the corner and disappear. We both needed to cool down. We both needed some space. We both knew things would heal.

As the stress of the moment drained away, so did my energy, and I needed to eat. With my head full of Elena, I sleepwalked round the kitchen and made two cheese sandwiches out of the stale loaf of bread. I crashed on the sofa with the food and pictured the flat being big enough for three. There were two decent bedrooms – one *could* be a nursery. I imagined it painted blue, with cars drawn on the walls and it filled with toys and games. Yes, it would be a good nursery.

I bit into my last half of sandwich and flicked on the TV, but couldn't get the baby off my mind. *How could I even consider getting rid of it? Or do anything to risk losing Elena? Yes, in a few months, my life will change, but I should celebrate that. I can love and protect my very own family, in my smart home, with my great job. Haven't I worked hard to deserve that?*

I turned off the TV and closed my eyes to appreciate the man I'd become.

FORTY-THREE

It was Tuesday 6th December and the partner's premeet again. I was keen to catch Elena before the meeting, to apologise for being a prick. I passed by her desk on my way to the boardroom, but she wasn't in.

I entered the near-full boardroom and, in the din of the premeet chatter, found my usual seat. I laid down my ordered papers and sat poised and ready to spar. Philip wandered in last and called us to order, settling in his throne at the head of the pack. Then, after his introductory pleasantries, he handed the meeting to me. I took the room through performance figures and my next quarter planning. Finance partner Tom challenged me about forecasts, but I held my ground and Philip sided with me. He caught me as I was leaving.

'I like what you did. Tackling Tom was brave.'

'We'll easily hit those figures. He needs more faith.'

'Without his wriggle room, how will he massage us partners, hey? Anyway, Friday we'll have lunch. There's something I'm hoping to tell you.'

'Really?' The promotion was on its way.

'Let's see, eh?'

I raced to tell Elena, but she still wasn't in.

'She's taking another sick day.' Viv, her manager, caught me looking.

'Thanks, I'll give her a ring.' I was due to meet with the team, so it would have to wait.

After the team debrief, I was straight into trading and then back-to-back with clients. Late afternoon, I remembered Elena and felt the growing urgency to call. I was about to ring when Philip sauntered over.

'Do you have plans for tonight?'

'Well—'

'It doesn't matter if you have. It's just that I'm meeting Derek over dinner. I wondered whether you'd join us. I'm happy to fly solo, but it's a chance for you to muscle in.' He winked. 'I guarantee it'll be a good evening.'

Derek was a senior partner and notoriously difficult to pin down and impress. This was a great opportunity. Then my mind switched to Elena, and Philip saw the dilemma playing out in my head.

'Honestly, don't worry about it. We can do it another time.'

'No, it's okay. I want to join you. You're right, it's a really good chance.' *Hell, why not. I'll make it up to Elena tomorrow. After all, what could be better for the baby's future than his old man getting a partnership?*

Philip and I worked until six thirty and then caught a cab to meet Derek at Henry's. We were shown to Derek's table, where he looked like he'd been drinking a while. His sable suit jacket gaped open and he'd pulled his tie off-centre. In the ice bucket sat a new bottle of wine. He smiled with his playful, hazel eyes and gestured for us to sit opposite. I'd wondered what he'd make of me tagging along, but he didn't show any surprise.

The evening was more my scene than jostling to impress in meetings. Over wine and a couple of brandies, we firmed our connection, swapping stories about our bravest, best trades. I had a long way to go to beat Derek, and his stories had us in stitches.

Derek drained his brandy glass then checked his watch. 'Is that the time? I'd better get off to Sally. What about you, Peter? Is there a little lady waiting at home?'

'He's far too smart for that,' Philip answered for me.

'Actually… that's where you're wrong,' I said.

'Oh? You've been holding out on me.' Philip nudged my arm.

'Elena's having our baby.'

'What a devil! You kept that quiet. Congratulations!' Philip took my hand and shook it.

'Great news, congratulations!' Derek stood and shook my hand too.

'I know, it's all happened so quickly. We're really pleased, of course.'

'I didn't think you wanted a family.' Philip smiled over to Derek. 'He's too obsessed with the job.'

'You've obviously met the right girl,' said Derek.

'I have.' And I meant it. I'd made my own family, where I finally belonged. But for some reason, I thought of Faye. Now I understood, exactly in that moment, the depth of all she'd lost. No one had been there for her. 'At least *I* never let her down.'

'No, you're a good man. You're doing the right thing.' Philip raised his glass.

'Oh.' I realised I'd spoken out loud.

'Waiter!' Derek clicked his fingers. 'A bottle of your finest Champagne!'

I landed home steaming drunk, and it was too late to

241

call Elena. Without processing any guilt, I collapsed into bed.

The next morning, my head throbbed out a faithful reminder of my bad old drinking ways. I treated myself to an extra hour of sleep and wagered that Philip would do the same.

At seven, I rolled out of the sheets and attacked my morning chores with a gusto that was fake, tricking myself into wellness. It sort of worked and my head stopped spinning.

As I prepared to leave, I looked over to where the rose had been. 'That silly rose. Why did I choose it over Elena?' It was a moment of madness and I felt ashamed. 'I don't need a crutch. I don't need your sorcery, Faye.'

Then I swear I heard laughter.

The phone rang and broke it.

'Hello, is this Peter?' a man's thick Italian accent asked.

'Yes, who's this?'

'My name's Raniero Milani. I'm Elena's father.'

He sounded serious, like a man hunting down the rogue who'd got his little girl pregnant. I chose to play dumb.

'It's taken me a couple of days to find your number.' *Here goes…* 'And I'm sorry to tell you this, but there's been an accident.'

'An accident?'

'Yes.'

'What sort of accident?'

'Sorry… I've been trying to reach you since Monday—'

'What accident? Where's Elena?'

'I'm afraid… She was hit by a car and… thank God. She wouldn't have felt a thing.'

242